Left Out

Left Out

M.M. Murray

ARCHWAY
PUBLISHING

Archway Publishing books may be ordered
through booksellers or by contacting:

Archway Publishing
1663 Liberty Drive
Bloomington, IN 47403
www.archwaypublishing.com
1 (888) 242-5904

ISBN: 978-1-4808-6318-7 (sc)
ISBN: 978-1-4808-6317-0 (e)

Library of Congress Control Number: 2018905836

Print information available on the last page.

Archway Publishing rev. date: 5/30/2018

Chapter 1

I heard the blonde one say, "Hey, here she comes." I squeezed into a crowd of kids who stood by their lockers in the corridor of our middle school. It was the third day of school, and after the first couple of times they banged into me, I started to look down at the floor for a foot that might shoot out to trip me. Then the assault came. Two elbows, one on each side, shoved me. I started to fall, but almost without thinking about it, my left foot planted itself on the floor and saved me. There were so many kids around that anyone standing close probably couldn't really tell if it was accidental or not. But I knew. I kept moving my feet toward social studies class.

At lunchtime I grabbed a tray and got in line. Whoever was behind me kept giving me little shoves. Once my tray was loaded, I turned and looked across the sea of faces. An achy feeling crawled into my chest, but I spotted an empty table far away from everybody near the wall. I walked toward it.

Suddenly, something caught my ankle, and I was falling forward. My tray with my lunch on it clanked on the tile floor, and everything on it slid across the shiny surface. Out of the corner of my eye, I saw a blue sneaker with red laces pull away fast—the same kind from this morning when I almost hit the lockers.

It got really embarrassing when two lunch ladies rushed over to help me. One grabbed my tray from the floor and brushed it off. The other wiped a cloth across the cellophane wrapper on my sandwich and placed it on the tray with my bag of chips and milk carton. I was able to stand up without their help. That was a good thing!

"There you go, hon. No harm done. Are you okay?"

"Yep, thanks." I turned away from the other kids' stares and headed to the table, set my tray down, and then sat with my back to everyone in the room. I forced each bite of sandwich down with a gulp of milk.

"What's going on? Why are those girls tripping you?" I turned around to look up at the voice behind me, but I was surprised to see a kid sitting in a wheelchair.

"What do you mean?" I asked.

"Hey, I'm Eden. Just moved here. Starting sixth grade. Anyway, I saw them this morning when I was waiting at the elevator and then just now. That blonde one and two of her minions tripped you." A woman holding a tray placed it on the table. "Thanks," he said, looking up at her. "I'm good here."

He didn't touch his food. Instead he glared at me, waiting for an answer. His eyes were full of concern.

"It's nothing," I said. "Must have been a mistake. I'm Abby. Starting grade six too." I chewed another bite of sandwich, hoping he would forget about what he saw.

"How long have they been doing this?" He finally took a bite of his sandwich. But he never took his eyes off me.

I decided to change the subject so I didn't have to talk about this. "So who do you have for teachers?"

"Let's see—Johnson for math, Gonzales for science, Pearson for social studies, and Haley for language arts. All pretty good so far, but it's early." He drew milk in through the straw.

"Pearson? I have her too. I haven't seen you in our class."

"Just started yesterday around noon. Was with my parents at a meeting with special ed most of the morning."

I looked at his face, especially his eyes. They were bright blue and had a lot of energy like the rest of his face. "So where did you move to?"

"Alston Street, number seventy-eight. Know where that is?"

"I should. That's next door to our house!"

He smiled wide. "Hey, cool, we're neighbors!"

"Yep, cool." I put my thumb up.

The bell rang for the end of lunch period. I offered to carry his tray over to the barrel, but he said he had it. He placed it on his knees and rolled his chair toward the doors, shoved the trash into the barrel, and plopped the tray into its receptacle, all in one easy move.

Before he left the cafeteria, he turned and said, "Hey, since we're neighbors, would you be okay with filling me in on what I missed with Pearson those first couple of days? My van drops me off around three." His eyes were filled with hope.

"Sure. Today?"

He nodded his head. "My bus gets to my house around 3:15, I think."

"See you then. Just come up the ramp to the deck."

I jumped off the school bus in front of my house and headed toward the ramp leading up to Eden's deck. The funny thing was that it used to be my best friend Shelly's house before she moved. If she still lived there, she'd be working with me on the project for social studies at school. I didn't know Eden that well yet, but I hoped he wanted to do the project together. If not, I couldn't think of anyone else to ask. That meant I would have to do the whole thing by myself and present it at the fair. I couldn't imagine doing that without Shelly.

From the top of the ramp, Eden shouted, "Hey, Abby!"

"Want to work on social studies project together?" I blurted out before I even said hello.

"You kidding? I heard about that in one of my other classes. I was hoping you'd ask that," Eden said. His eyes widened. "Cool! Come on up." He pulled his wheelchair back to let me by. "Let's work in the kitchen. What were you thinking of doing? Hey, have some of my mom's world-renowned cookies and lemonade." He pointed to the table. I sat down and picked a cookie while he poured some lemonade for me.

"I didn't decide yet."

That morning, Ms. Pearson reviewed the directions for the project. We would have about six weeks to get ready to show it at the social studies fair. Since we were on Egypt, we had to choose a topic about Egyptian life, something like food, clothing, sanitation, or transportation, and find new information about it. Once we decided that, we had to figure out the best way to present our information. "You can make a diorama or a chart with information or create a game with facts about the topic, or you can dress in the clothing of the time and allow people to ask you questions," Ms. Pearson had said. "How you do it is up to you. You can work alone or in a group. Keep in mind that deciding to work alone won't necessarily get you a better grade and vice versa. Each individual has to show how he or she contributed to the project."

"I'll bet most kids are probably going to do the usual things like foods or transportation, maybe clothing," he said. "I'd like to do something where we can find some new things that we haven't covered in class. You know, different."

"Yeah, I get it. Not just saying stuff everybody already knows." My brain started to buzz. "But it has to be something we can find good information on. We don't have a lot of time. What about something like if we grew up in Egypt, then how different would our lives be?"

"But doesn't that just lead us back to things like clothes, food, and transportation?"

"Not if we think about things that you can't see but still make a difference," I said.

"Like what?" Eden sat up straight and clicked the button on his pen fast as if it helped him to think.

"Like rules or making money, something like that."

"Okay, let's go with rules. Like school rules?" Eden asked.

"It could mean that, but that might be hard to find out about in the time we have to do this. It's more about whether people there had rights like we do and if their rules were like ours," I answered. I laid my pad on the table and started to write our ideas. In my mind, though, I saw myself fall in the school corridor. It felt like someone's foot blocked my ankle as I was walking.

"Like how did they make laws, and then who enforced them?" Eden added.

"Yeah, we could start there. Then we could pick some rules we have now and see if they had rules or laws like that back then. Like rules for driving. We have cars, but they had carts drawn by horses. Did they have to follow rules on the roads? Or maybe trying to sell something. You know, like did regular people back then have choices about what they could do, and who said they did?" I tapped my pencil against the table.

"And if you broke the law, what happened?" Eden's face was alive with energy.

"Did you get a lawyer to help you," I offered, "or did you just go to jail? And who decided how long you stayed there?" The ideas poured out of me.

"This is cool, Abby. Maybe we could talk about how people made money and who decided how much you got paid like a salary. Or did people get a salary?"

"That's another topic, but it seems like too much to do both ideas," I said.

"Hey, why don't we go online and see what we find about each topic. That might help us decide." Eden pulled his laptop closer. His fingers tapped the keys until the web page appeared.

We spent the next hour exploring each topic. We were so involved in what we were doing that we lost touch with everything around us. Then Eden's mother came into the kitchen to start supper. We both looked up at the kitchen window, now covered in black.

"Hey, you two. You going to stop for food?"

"Hey, Mom, I don't think you met Abby. Guess what? She lives next door."

"Hello, Abby. I think you're the first neighbor we've met."

"Hi. Nice to meet you."

"Abby is in my social studies class, and we're gonna do the project together for the fair."

"Sounds like a good plan, especially since you both live so close to each other. It should make it easier to work on it." She placed the empty plate and lemonade pitcher in the dishwasher.

"Let's get together tomorrow and finish these ideas," Eden said.

"Okay. Let's keep looking for things on our topics tonight. I'd better get going. My mom likes me to be there when she and Dad get home from work. Bye, Mrs. Gray."

"Bye, Abby. See you tomorrow."

"Yep." I looked over at Eden. "See you at lunch."

As I walked down the ramp to my house, a sinking feeling poured over me, pushing all the brightness out. I knew what it was—Stephanie, the blonde one who helped trip me.

Chapter 2

The next day as my math teacher, Mr. Gibson, was checking my homework, he asked, "So Abby, did the way I showed how to do this yesterday make it easier to do?"

I always had a hard time telling a lie because you had to keep all the details straight in your head. Rather than mess up and make a mistake, I told the truth. "No," I squeaked out. My stomach started to churn. I waited. Would he embarrass me?

"So, you did it another way?"

"Yes."

"Can you explain how you got your answer then if you didn't do it the way I showed you?" Even when he talked to just one student, his voice was loud. He didn't sound mad when he said it, but there was something in his voice—not a challenge really but almost. He moved his glasses onto the top of his head and crossed his arms over his chest waiting for me to say something. Suddenly, the room got quiet. I couldn't see them, but I knew every set of eyes in the room was burning holes in my head from all sides. I froze. *Me? Explain myself?* No way could I explain something out loud in front of people, especially to kids in my class. Not going to happen. My face got very hot. It probably matched my red T-shirt. If only I could be a speck of dust on the floor, somewhere low, anywhere in this room but in my seat.

"No," I answered, "I, I can't."

A look crossed Mr. Gibson's face that I couldn't figure out. Was it anger or disappointment? Whatever it was, things did not look good for me.

"In order to get extra credit, you have to be able to explain how you got your answer." He stood and waited for me to speak.

Does he think I copied my answer? He doesn't understand. I don't need to copy anyone's work! I got the answer myself. Why can't the floor open so I could fall through? There was no way to escape. I lowered my head, tucked my hands into my lap, and held my pencil tight like it was a lifeline that could lift me out of this embarrassing moment. I looked over my shoulder at Stephanie, one of the four who had tripped me twice. She looked back at me with this grin on her face.

"Does anyone who did it a different way want to share how they did it?" Mr. Gibson asked. Out of the corner of my eye, I saw hands flapping in the air. Of course, one of them was Stephanie's. Mr. Gibson turned away from me.

The pain from that embarrassment followed me all day long from one class to the next. Fortunately, not all the kids in my math class were in my other classes, except for Stephanie. I was sure she took in the whole thing. I silently told God I would never complain to my mother again about having to eat lima beans if he would keep Gibson from saying anything when he checked my work again. That was a pretty big bargain because my mother had lima beans for supper at least twice a month.

The funny thing is that I like math. I understand it. I always thought that the important thing in math was getting the right answer. Usually, I come up with other ways that are faster to solve the problem without using the teacher's way. But I guess that doesn't count. Now I know that if I can't explain the way I got my answer, I'd better do it Mr. Gibson's way.

✻ ✻ ✻

When I got home from school, I shut my bedroom door, flopped on my bed, and propped a pillow behind me. My stuffed animals crowded around me. It was a good thing I like my room because since my best friend Shelly had left, I spent of lot of time here when I wasn't in school. The dark purple walls were peaceful. I grabbed Ralph, my stuffed rhinoceros, and held him close to my chest.

Mr. Gibson is a turd, I thought. *That's all there is to it. Doesn't he know you're not supposed to embarrass kids. Good teachers don't do that. I pay attention in class and do my homework. It's not fair. He embarrassed me in front of all the other kids. Why should I try hard for him if he's going to treat me that way?*

This picture of me riding a real rhino into Mr. Gibson's class flew into my head. I could just see the look on his face as he thought about challenging me in front of the other kids. Tomorrow had to be better or … or what? Or nothing! There was nothing I could do to change things.

I looked up at the giant poster on the wall—a birthday present from Shelly. It showed Wonder Woman, who uses all kinds of magical powers on bad guys. Her hair was a lot like mine, a bunch of tight curls but a lot longer. What I liked best about her, though, were her eyes. They were fierce and strong like the bulging muscles in her arms and legs. No one would mess with her! I wished I could be like that.

❋ ❋ ❋

"Abby, Mom and I are going golfing. We'll be back by five or so." My father stood in the doorway to my bedroom. "You okay? Need anything?" It was noontime on Saturday, their time to "get out and do something relaxing."

"No, I'm okay," I said, wishing they would teach me how to play golf. Then I could be with them on Saturday afternoons.

"If we don't get going, we're going to miss our tee time," my mother yelled from downstairs.

"I'll keep my cell on if you need us," he said. He sounded like he didn't want to leave me behind.

"Okay."

I liked and hated weekends at the same time. I liked the weekend because I didn't have to be in school, especially math class. Not having Shelly to hang with sucked though.

Through the half-open window, I heard a door slide and a strange whirring sound that reminded me of my dad's electric drill. It stopped and started, stopped and started several times. Then all of a sudden, I heard this rumbling like a bike going over a wooden bridge. I rushed to the window and saw Eden going down the ramp at the side of the house on his wheelchair.

"So, what do you think?" his father asked. "How does it feel? Better than the other one?"

"Oh, man, Dad, this is so cool! It's like riding a bike except I don't have to pedal. Hey, how fast do you think this thing goes?" All I could see was his cap sliding along the top of the bushes between our houses.

"Okay," his father said, "just so we're clear, you have to follow some speed rules. Inside two miles an hour, and outside five. And most important, no wheelies."

"That's pretty funny, Dad. If I could do wheelies, I probably wouldn't need this thing." He did a few circles in the driveway and then shot back up the ramp. "Wha-hoo!" he yelled when he turned the chair around and drove it back down.

"Eden, easy does it," his father said.

"Yeah, okay, no wheelies and slow like a turtle." He slowed the chair so it was hardly moving. "How's this, Dad? Slow … slow … hardly moving." He stopped the chair. "What's the point of having a motor if you can't go fast?"

"The point is to take some of the pressure off your back muscles."

"Got it. Hey, can I stay out here for a while and practice?"

"If I hear any more hoots, I'll be back out," his father said.

"Yeah, I can race down the ramp without yelling."

"Ever heard of a governor?" his father asked.

"Yeah, it's someone who's in charge of a state."

"That's the person. I'm talking about the thing."

"What's it for?"

"You attach it to a motor to control it. Understand where I'm going with this?"

"Yeah, Dad, don't worry. No governor."

His father walked up the ramp and into the house. All I heard after that was the whirring of the chair and the rumble of the tires. I had only known Eden a few days at this point, but I sure liked his spirit. In fact, he reminded me a lot of Shelly. She always had a positive way of looking at things. I suppose I could send her an email to find out how she's doing. I sat at my computer to write her a quick message.

✻ ✻ ✻

About five o'clock, a car pulled into the driveway. My parents were back.

"Abby, I need you down here to help with supper," my mother yelled from downstairs.

When I walked into the kitchen, my mother said, "Snap the ends off those beans please."

I grabbed a small sharp knife and stood at the sink to work on the string beans.

"So, what did you do this afternoon?" my mother asked as she spread flour over a paper towel.

"Worked on my project for social studies."

"Didn't you go outside like I suggested? Honestly, Abby, it wouldn't hurt to get some sun on your face. You look so pale." She dipped pieces of chicken into flour.

If I didn't change the subject, she would stay on it. "Guess what? Eden has a new wheelchair."

"Oh, did you see him this afternoon?"

"No, he was with his father practicing how to use it."

"Why didn't you go over to say hello?"

"I was kind of busy with homework. I'll probably see him tomorrow."

"Well, I think you missed a perfectly good opportunity to get out of the house and into the fresh air. You should try to be more outgoing, Abby." She set the meat in the hot oil, and it sizzled back like it was angry. "Tell me why you didn't go over."

"I don't know. I guess I just wanted to get my homework done."

"I can see how you might not want to play with a

friend who lives in a wheelchair, but it could be temporary, maybe a broken leg. Let's hope it's not something permanent."

"Yeah, I guess it would be hard to play with someone who lives in a wheelchair," I said. Sometimes I would get really sarcastic with my mother, but I couldn't help it. She brought it out in me.

"Abby, that's ridiculous," she shot back. "You'll never be popular unless you put yourself out there. All you ever do is sit up there at that computer, working on homework. When I was your age, my mother pushed me out the door as soon as I got home from school. I had to make friends, or I would have been totally on my own."

"What do you expect me to do, Mom?"

"Go out with your friends, go to the mall. That's where you meet other kids your age." She poked the meat with her fork making loud taps every time it hit the pan, kind of like a drumbeat. Maybe that helped get her point across.

"Yeah, all the kids that I would really like to be friends with. Besides, you have to dress a certain way to even talk to them." Instead of picking up the beans one at a time, I stabbed them with the knife as I spoke. It was like we had this mini concert of anger going on—all percussion instruments.

"What does this have to do with your clothes?" my mother asked.

I wanted to say, "The kids at school make fun of them," but instead I said, "Nothing." According to her way of looking at things, it would end up being my fault. I sprayed the beans and then aimed the water in the corner of the sink and let it shoot out full force. It rushed up the side of the sink and showered onto the counter. Fortunately, my mother was not looking my way. I tore off a piece of paper towel and mopped up the pool of water.

A small cloud of steam rose above the frying pan when she added water.

"Put those in the steamer with water and set the timer for twenty minutes. Dinner will be ready in half an hour. Don't forget to set the table before you go back upstairs."

That meant she was going in to have a drink with dad and she did not want me there. After setting the table, I climbed the stairs and sat down at my computer.

Sometimes I wondered what other kids did on weekends. When Shelly was here, she often had to leave my house early on Saturday afternoon because her parents were taking her and her brother out for supper somewhere or to a movie. She said sometimes they would play board games after supper or watch a movie. Other than helping to get supper ready and eating, I spent almost no time with my parents. Not because I didn't want to but because whenever I tried to join them, my mother looked up at me and said something like, "Don't you have some homework to do, Abby?" or, "You must have something to keep you busy up in your room."

The final blow came one day about two weeks ago when she said to me, "Honestly, Abby, ever since Shelly moved, you've been so clingy. I wish you'd find a new friend."

My father shot a look at her when she said that. He must have been as surprised as I was. "I don't see any reason Abby can't sit with us for a while," he said.

If my father had a motto, it would probably be "Don't rock the boat." He turned to me and said, "Abs, I'll be up later to check on you."

I wasn't totally deprived, of course. Like the other day when I knew he was in the basement at his workbench, I went down to join him. "Hey, what are you up to? Need to make something?" he said.

"No, I just want to see what you're doing."

He had a doorknob in his hands. "Trying to figure out why this doesn't work all of a sudden. Guess it just needs a little oil. You know, I was thinking about getting my boat out and spending some time this winter sprucing it up for spring."

It was hard for me to keep my hands still when I was at his workbench, so I drilled holes in a piece of scrap wood. My dad had taught me how to use the drill one time, and ever since, I practiced drilling whenever I was with him at his workbench.

"So, whenever you have time, you can help me."

"Yeah, cool."

One good thing about my dad was he'd show me how to use his tools. It wasn't because he wished he had a son or anything. He just seemed to like having me around him. Since I liked to make things, we were a good pair.

Chapter 3

After school I left most of my books on our back stairs and walked across the lawn to Eden's. As my shoes clomped up the ramp, Eden shouted down to me, "That you, Abby?"

"Yep."

"Hey, we've got more cookies."

I smiled when I got to the top of the ramp and sat in the chair facing him. "That's for you." He pointed to a glass of lemonade.

"Thanks." As I sipped, I looked at Eden. He must have figured out that there was a question behind my eyes because he swallowed what he was chewing and looked back at me.

"What?" he asked. His shoulders pitched forward.

"Nothing. I was just thinking." I looked away from him and sipped more of my drink.

"About what? Come on, Abby. Remember what I said yesterday. I can't get to know you unless you talk."

"Yeah. Except I don't know if I should ask it." I

twirled my straw. "I mean, what if it's something you don't want to talk about?"

"Then I'll tell you." Eden sat back and took another bite of his cookie.

"What happened to you?" Man, I really had to do a better job of thinking about my questions before letting them shoot out of my mouth.

"You mean to land me in this chair?"

I nodded and squirmed but kept my eyes on him.

"It's okay. Most people don't bother to ask. I guess they don't want to know." Eden put his hands around his thighs as if he suddenly became aware of his legs. "What happened was that when I was about six, I started to stumble around when I was walking. Then I would walk like a duck almost, you know, instead of bending my knees. After that, I had trouble getting upstairs, and it was hard to push things like a bike or a wagon. At first, my parents just thought I was clumsy, so they didn't make anything of it, but when it got worse, they took me to a doctor. The tests they gave me showed I have muscular dystrophy. Ever heard of it?"

"Yes, but I don't know what it is." What amazed me was how calm he was as he talked about it as if it was some small thing.

"It's like your muscles get weaker as you get older, then they can't support you. That's why I need this chair. Guess I'll be in it for …" He looked away from me and finished by saying, "Forever." His eyes flickered as if thinking about it caused him pain. "They give me therapy so my muscles won't become like jelly, I guess. They're trying to keep them working as long as they can." He looked back at me. "So that's how I got here." This time Eden slapped the arms of his wheelchair. "So, what do you think?"

The question surprised me. I tried to put myself in his place. I felt bad for him but didn't want to make him feel depressed, so I said, "Thanks for telling me."

"Thanks for asking. I had a pretty good day." Eden took another cookie and offered the plate to me. "So enough about me. What's going on with you and those kids who tripped you?"

"What do you mean?"

"Why are they after you?" Eden asked, looking right into my face.

I took a long sip of lemonade, trying to think of a good way to get out of talking about this. "There's nothing going on. It was … you know, an accident."

"An accident, Abby? Come on. The same group both times?"

"I didn't notice who it was. It was nothing, really." Right now, I needed to get away from his talking about the tripping. I wasn't sure how he would take it, but I said, "Do you mind if we forget about that for now and work on our project? We have a lot of work to do and not a lot of time."

"For now, okay. But I'm not gonna forget about it. You have to tell me what's going on sometime soon, so we can figure out what to do. Right?"

I looked away from him but did not say anything.

"So, Egypt," he said. "Let's talk about what they would do when they had a problem." I knew he was trying to tease me, so I let a smile slide across my face.

Chapter 4

In social studies, Ms. Pearson handed back our compositions. Halfway down the page, I noticed a comment that said, "Nice thinking here." On the second page, she wrote, "You backed up your point well here. Good job!" An "A" was scrawled above another comment at the bottom of the page. "Nice job! You have good ideas. Let us hear more from you in class."

An "A" and great comments—that was so cool! But I'd probably never say anything in class. I'd never take the chance of looking dumb in front of *them*. Besides, I was better at writing my ideas than saying them out loud. When I wrote an answer, I could go at my own speed. But when I had to say an answer, when I had to put it altogether in order in my head fast before the teacher picked another kid, I would get all tongue-tied. If I could get credit for just writing my ideas down instead of having to say them, I would probably get an A for a final grade in all of my classes.

Is it possible that your hands can feel happy? That was

how mine felt as I carefully slid my composition into my backpack between two stiff books so it wouldn't get wrinkled. *Can't wait to show it to …* I was going to say Shelly. I did it again. I forgot she's gone. I could email her about it, but even if she sent a happy response, it wasn't the same as looking right into your friend's face when she was wearing a big smile because she was happy for you. I wasn't sure I knew Eden well enough to talk about grades with him. But maybe, especially now that we were working together on the social studies project.

✳ ✳ ✳

Eden and I met again on his deck and talked about our project.

"I had a pretty good day." Eden took another cookie and offered the plate to me. "I think I'm getting to know some of the kids in my classes. How was it for you today?"

"It was good. I only got shoved twice." How did that slip out? My face got very hot.

"Shoved! Who shoved you? Same ones?" Eden stopped eating. His voice changed. It got low and became hard.

"Forget it. I didn't mean to say anything. It's

nothing." I sipped my soda and wrapped my hands around the glass, hoping it would cool me off.

"Hey, Abby, I shared with you the other day. Now it's your turn. Why are they shoving you around?" He bent forward in his chair, trying to lock eyes with me.

"I wish I knew." Suddenly, tears rolled across the edges if my eyes. I lowered my face so Eden wouldn't see them, but when I tilted my head, they slid down my cheeks. "I really don't know why they do it. I've tried to figure it out, but I can't." What I was saying sounded mushy. "When I come anywhere near them, they do something to me." I brushed a tear from the side of my cheek

"The same ones I saw the other day? Am I right about that, Abby?" Eden's gaze was pretty intense.

"Yes, Stephanie from social studies and three others." I took in some air, trying to calm myself down. It didn't help. "They travel together like a pack. One's in my language arts class. But Stephanie's, like, the leader, does the most talking.

"Did you tell a teacher?" Eden asked.

My head started to ache. "If I do that, it'll get worse."

"What do you mean?"

"They'll find other ways to get back at me." Good thing the sun was in my eyes because it gave me an excuse to turn my head away from Eden and rub my forehead, which was starting to ache.

"How do you know?" He was doing it again, being … persistent.

"Just a feeling. I can't explain it."

"So, you're gonna just let them do this to you all through middle school?"

"What else can I do about it?" Eden's anger surprised me, kind of gave me courage.

"I don't know. Hit back."

That did not sound like a very good idea! "Yeah, and then you know who will get in trouble? Not them, me. They would all gang up against me and lie to protect one another."

"You're probably right. But you can't let them do this for the next three years." For a moment, everything was quiet. I felt like I could hear the thoughts bouncing around inside Eden's head. "What did your parents say about it?"

"They don't know." I really did not want to go there.

Eden's eyebrows poked up in the middle. "You didn't tell them. Why?"

Again, he just plowed right in. Instead of answering, I lifted my shoulders and let them drop. Then I decided he deserved a better answer, so I said, "I don't know. I guess I thought they'd probably tell the principal, and that wouldn't help."

"Yeah, maybe you're right. Sometimes parents mess things up."

I sighed. Good. He wasn't going to talk me out of that.

"Well, come on, Abby. We've got to figure a way out of this. Let's see. How about putting some stink bombs in their lockers? No, no, if they traced that back to you, you'd probably get expelled." Eden was looking up at the sun as I sat staring at him with my mouth open. Then he laughed and faced his palms toward me. "Just joking, just joking. Sorry. Sometimes I do that when things get too serious. Okay, so when you get shoved, is it usually when the four of them are together, or does it happen sometimes when you see them by themselves?"

"I'm not sure. I think they're usually together, but I never stop to see who's there, I just keep going so I can get away from them fast."

"That's smart. But tomorrow if it happens, turn around and look to see if it's all of them or maybe one or two."

"You mean *when* it happens. Okay, I'll try," I said, unsure of what difference it would make.

"And see if Stephanie is always there. If she is,

maybe it only happens when she gives the order. Maybe the others only do it when she says to."

After talking about it, I had to admit I felt better. At least Eden took it seriously. I wanted to talk to my mother about it, but I was afraid she would blame it on me.

✳ ✳ ✳

"Have you met the new neighbor? Is she in your grade?" my father asked at supper that night.

"I met him, and he's in sixth grade and in my social studies class."

"It's a boy. How did you meet him?" my mother asked, handing me the dish of vegetables.

"In the lunchroom at school. He pulled his wheelchair up to my table."

"I don't think you ever explained why he's in a wheelchair. Is he injured?" my mother asked.

"No, he's disabled." My dad piled meat on my plate. He knew I liked meat better than vegetables.

"Oh, my! Did you talk to him about that?" she asked.

"He has muscular dystrophy," I spooned a few carrots onto my plate. Those were definitely not my favorite vegetable.

"Heavens," my mother said. "It might be difficult to become friends with someone who can't get around very well."

"What do you mean?" I waited for one of her off-the-wall reasons to fall out of her mouth.

"I don't know, Abby. It just seems like it might be difficult to plan things to do together."

"He can get around fine in his chair, Mom. And he can do a lot of things that most kids can do. He has trouble walking. That's all."

"Well, it doesn't seem very promising for you. You and Shelly spent most of your time running around the neighborhood together. This is going to be a big adjustment for you."

"Yeah, I know. But middle school has a lot more homework so I don't have time to run around. Eden and I spend time on homework and I like having someone to talk about school stuff with. I like that better than running around." I sighed. "Besides, didn't you tell me to get out and make friends? I did. Now you're telling me all the reasons you think I shouldn't spend time with someone."

"All I'm saying, Abby, is that you need friends you can get out and do things with, not spend all your time on homework. It seems like you're shutting yourself off from some other opportunities that might be good for you."

"Carol, Abby's best friend moved away. She connected with this young man, and they seem to enjoy each other's company. Where's the problem?" my father said. So, he agreed with me.

"All I'm saying is this doesn't sound like the best situation for Abby."

"Most kids see his wheelchair and probably think that he can't do a lot of physical things so why try to make friends with him. Abby was different. She did not see that as a negative," my father said. "On top of that, he's new to the area. That in itself is hard on kids."

"You two can think what you want, but I don't think this has much of a future."

"For now, Abby and Eden seem to get along fine. That does not mean she will never make other friends. We should be satisfied with this," my father said.

My mother glared at me, shook her head, and then returned to eating her food. At times like this, I ended up thinking that maybe there was a mix-up at the hospital and that I was sent home with the wrong mother.

* * *

That night as I worked on my language arts homework, my mind went back to what Eden said about Stephanie. What if he was right and Stephanie was responsible for getting the other kids to push me around? How could knowing that help? And why did she want to pick on me anyway? If we never knew each other before this, why would I be such an issue for her? Maybe she was just plain mean and needed a target, and that happened to be me.

I'd bet if I was tall with long hair and wore really cool clothes, they would leave me alone. Or if I was one of those kids who always had something smart to say in class, they would want me to be part of their group. Then I think, *Yuck! No way I want to act like them just to fit in.*

But I had to admit I wouldn't mind having more friends in school. Shelly and I were so happy being friends that we never bothered to invite other people to play with us. It wasn't that we were mean. It was just that we were, like, enough for each other. Maybe that was a mistake, but to be honest, I couldn't imagine being friends with some of the other girls in our class last year. Mostly they were like the pack—pretty, pushy, and perfect. At least that was what they thought.

For now, I had Eden to eat lunch with. For that

part of the day anyway, I'd be safe from them. At least I thought so!

❋ ❋ ❋

The cafeteria line crawled along. Eden's helper or para (which was short for something but I didn't know what) was pushing his chair against the end of an empty table. She crouched over him and said something. He laughed, and then she patted him on the shoulder and left the room. *Good. He's by himself.* I put my meal and a container of milk on my tray and walked toward him.

He looked up. "Hey, Abby, sit." He pointed to a chair. "As you can see, plenty of room."

"Yeah, so I see."

"So, anything happen today? You know, with the shoving?" he asked.

"Not so far. But we still have two hours left." I set my tray down.

"Hey, I think I saw them on the other side of the room." He looked around the cafeteria.

I put my sandwich up to my mouth and talked into it. "Yes, over by the windows. The table under the clock."

Eden took a few bites of his food and then lifted his head as he chewed. "I recognize two of them from my classes," he said. "The blonde one and the one with the long brown hair. Haven't heard either one of them say anything in class that was, like, inspiring. But I haven't been here that long, so I'll let you know. I wonder what it is about you that bothers them."

"Maybe they don't need a reason. Maybe they just choose someone who looks easy to pick on, who looks like she won't fight back," I said.

"You could be right. Hey, here they come. Right toward us." Eden stopped eating and sat up straight as he stared at the four girls who walked directly toward us. He kept his eyes on Stephanie as she led the others right past our table. She turned her head and looked straight at him, and he locked eyes with her. *Man, he's not afraid of them.* "Hey, guys, any reason you need to come all the way over here to get out of the cafeteria? The door was pretty close to where you were sitting."

I pushed my face into my sandwich and prayed he wouldn't say anything else to get them upset.

Stephanie stopped, turned toward him, and did that thing with her head that made her head move like those bobble-head dolls that people put on their car dashboard. "Yeah, wobbly legs, we wanted to see what people with small brains talk about at lunch. Nothing worth thinking about, I guess."

"Takes someone with a small brain to care about something like that," he said. "I always thought that was the category you guys would fall into." He turned his chair toward her and smiled wide. She turned on her heel, and the other three followed her out of the room.

"So that's the pack," he said after they passed.

"Yep, all four of them." My heart was beating so rapidly I thought it would jump out of my chest. "I thought they might do something just then," I said. "That was close." I took a breath and let it out.

"Naw, too public," Eden answered. "They wouldn't risk being caught picking on a kid in a wheelchair."

"The corridors are public too," I said, looking at him.

"Yeah, but there's so many kids that they can get away with saying something was an accident." Eden continued, "I was thinking. Is there any way you can get to class without running in to them?"

"How?"

"Like, go a different way." Eden talked in between bites. For a skinny kid, he sure loved to eat.

"I thought about that, but I figured I might be late

for class." I was hungry before we started talking. Now my sandwich stared back at me.

"Have you tried it?"

"No." My throat tightened.

"Tell you what. Today, when you come over after school, let's look at the map of the school in the student handbook. Maybe we can work it out."

When he suggested that, I relaxed and smiled. Then my stomach growled. I wrapped my fingers around the sandwich bun and took a huge bite.

Mr. Gibson was checking our math homework at the beginning of class. He approached my desk and picked up my homework. I felt him standing next to me and heard the tap of his pencil against his clipboard as he checked the answer to each of the math problems on my paper. He flipped through the papers and then turned them over as if something else should have been there. Then his forehead wrinkled. Was he puzzled? He looked over at me. I held my breath and waited for the comment, always loud enough for everyone to hear. Would it be embarrassing or not? "Well, you seem to be catching on, Abby. I guess you've finally figured out how the formula works." It seemed like he was going to say something else. Instead he kind of nodded and then laid my papers down and moved on to the next student.

Actually, I didn't use his formula. I solved the problems my way first, which was three times faster. Then I rewrote them using his formula. That was the only way to please him. Even though I always get the answers right doing it my way, my first experience with him told me to follow his procedure or get a lower grade. I guess you don't get credit in Mr. Gibson's math class for being creative.

When he approached Stephanie, a smile was plastered from one side of his face to the other as he went through her homework. "As usual, Stephanie, nicely done."

Stephanie returned his smile. "Thanks, Mr. G." When he passed, she made a motion with her eyes the way I did sometimes when my mother said something I thought was way out there.

If only Mr. Gibson could hear her comments about him outside of class. One time I heard her say, "With what he knows about math, he couldn't get a real job." But the way she acted toward him in class showed she really knew how to get on his good side.

After class I walked ahead of Stephanie, who talked to another girl loud enough for me to hear her. "So, she finally figured out how to do the problems. Man, I can't imagine what it's like to be that dumb." They both giggled. I knew the comment was meant for me. It hurt more than the embarrassment of being pushed or tripped. I wasn't sure why. Maybe because it seemed like most kids looked up to other kids who acted smart in class and did things the right way. People thought they were special. They sure didn't think that about me. What bugged me about that was those *smart* kids weren't always that smart. They just acted like they were. Like, for instance, in social studies they could tell you all the facts about any event that was being discussed, but if someone asked them to explain what caused it, they couldn't do it. That was the stuff that interested me. Facts didn't explain events. They just, like, put labels on them. Almost anyone could do that.

I picked up speed to get away from them and almost collided with another student as we entered language arts.

"Sorry," I said.

"It's okay," the girl replied.

Language arts was different from math in a lot of ways. For one thing, the teacher wanted us to think about what we read and to come up with some different ways of looking at ideas about it. We often worked in small groups. A small group was easier for me. It was private. Another good thing about it was that there wasn't one way to solve a problem we were discussing with the teacher. Whatever you said could be a possible solution as long as you could explain yourself. So, I didn't feel as stupid here as I did in math. Once in a while, one of the kids in our group might say something funny, and we would all laugh. I liked that because if I was the one who just said something, I knew they were laughing with me, not at me. It made me feel warm, accepted, I guess.

Another reason I did better here was I could write my ideas down before I said them. That helped me to sort things out and then put them in order so it made sense to me. Then I reread them the way I wrote them and fixed the comments up until they sounded right to me. Once I did that, I didn't mind sharing my ideas out loud. Besides, my language arts teacher, Ms. Lawler, was cool. She joked a lot and laughed with us.

"All right, people, let's get started. Last night for homework, you all did a superlative job, I'm sure, writing your thoughts about how Peter does or does not fit the view of a hero that we came up with yesterday, right?" She lowered her glasses and scanned the room to see our faces.

"Ms. Lawler," one of the boys asked, "what does superlative mean?"

"The first part of the word should give you a hint, John," she said, looking over at him.

"Su-per, super, oh yeah, I did a superlative job." He turned, smiled wide, and stuck his thumb up in the air, and the kids in his group laughed.

"As, I'm sure, all of your classmates did. Am I right, ladies and gentlemen?"

Across the room you could hear agreement as we repeated the word superlative several times and then smiled back at Ms. Lawler. "You see how that works? I expect you to do superlative work, then you do it. It's that easy."

"Not always, Ms. Lawler," another boy said. "Sometimes the assignments are hard."

"But Paulo, it's my job to stretch your mind," she said, cocking her head a little and holding her hands out face up like she was pleading for understanding.

"Yeah, and you're *superlative* at it, Ms. Lawler." Laughter erupted once again. "The only thing is— sometimes you make us do so much thinking that I feel like any minute my brain's gonna snap like a rubber band that someone stretches too far."

"Paulo, that was a *very* nice simile. And using the word superlative in a sentence," she said and patted her chest, "Oh my, too much excitement for this teacher for one day."

"Yeah, thanks, Ms. Lawler. Anything I can do to help."

That was what it was like in language arts. We did a lot of thinking, but we also laughed. I was definitely more relaxed here. Plus, I really liked the things we discuss. Why couldn't all the classes be this way?

Chapter 5

The rain pelted the deck outside. Eden and I sat at his kitchen table with the student handbook on the table in front of us. His pencil raced back and forth across a pad of paper as he drew grid lines to make a chart for the days of the week. He was creating a plan to help me avoid the pack during school.

"Okay, now let's put your classes in for Mondays starting with homeroom. Where do you go after that?"

"Language arts, room 221."

"Do you meet them on your way there?"

"Usually."

"Okay, if you go down this stairway," he said and pointed to the school map, "and then come up this one, you should avoid them. After language arts, where do you go?"

"Math, room 226."

We worked out a plan for Monday only and decided that I would try it out before doing any other days. "Do you think it might work?" Eden sounded hopeful.

"It might," I said. "I'll let you know after school on Monday. You know what I worry about though? How long is it going to take them to figure out what's going on? Or will I get into trouble when I bump into the principal in the hallway downstairs running between the stairways?"

"Maybe, but it's worth trying, isn't it?"

Eden's enthusiasm reminded me of this exhibit I saw once at the science museum where electrical bolts snapped and crackled back and forth between two poles. That was what it was like to work with him. He was kind of electrically charged. I had to admit, though, I wasn't sure his plan would work. He was trying so hard to help me, but when it came to bravery, I had, like, none. Eden had enough for ten people. Truth was that I'd rather give in than fight. Maybe he was right. Maybe it was time to fight back, stick up for myself. I looked at Eden. "Yeah, it's really worth it. Thanks for helping." I smiled at him, and he lifted the plate of cookies.

"Better bulk up."

I took two cookies, and we sat back in our chairs and talked about our classes.

* * *

On Saturday afternoon my parents were off to the golf course again. I pushed against the bed pillow and balanced my books on my lap. Hard as I tried to push out the thoughts about the experiment Eden and I had planned for Monday, there were some questions I had to figure out the answers to ahead of time. For sure, I had to have an answer ready in case a teacher or the principal stopped me in the lower hallway on the way to my next class.

Okay, first, they'd probably ask what I was doing on that corridor if my class was upstairs. I could say, "I got lost." No, it was too late in the year for that. I wondered if they'd believe me saying, "I'm dropping a note off to a teacher." They could check that one out. Maybe I could say I had a hard time getting around the crowd in the hallway or I had to go to the office. Whatever I said had to sound believable. This plan had a lot of holes in it, but I had to try it out.

* * *

On Monday, I arrived in homeroom with my stomach fluttering. It was day one of the experiment. Since I wouldn't get back to my locker until lunchtime,

I loaded all the books I'd need for my morning classes into one pile. Running upstairs with all this extra weight was not going to be easy, but I had no choice. When the bell to change classes sounded, I held back until two of *them* moved away from me down the corridor. I scooted to the left, pushed the stairway door open, and took the stairs down to the first floor. Before stepping into the corridor, I looked both ways. Deserted! My arms ached under the weight of the extra books, and my breathing was heavy. Beneath me, my legs refused to hurry. Once inside the stairwell, I stopped for a few quick breaths then and pushed each foot against the stairs, taking one at a time. Slowly, my body with all the books went up. If muscles could talk, I'll bet mine would have cried for help under all that weight. At least that was what the aching in my legs told me.

Finally, I pulled open the door at the top of the stairs and walked directly across to my classroom. I'd made it! I sank into my chair, put my pile of books on the table, and waited for my heartbeat to slow down. I would have to do this two more times before lunch. There was no way I was gonna make it! Forty minutes later I was only half aware of what we had done in class.

The signal to change classes again startled me.

Once most of the kids had left class, I checked Eden's schedule and crossed over to the stairway to begin my route all over again. When I opened the door at the bottom of the stairwell, however, I found myself in the middle of a class change in that corridor. We forgot to think about the different schedules in seventh and eighth grades.

"Hey, squirt, watch where you're going," one kid yelled down at me when I bumped into him. The larger bodies of the seventh graders pressing against me made it twice as hard to get to the stairway. Finally, I arrived. Man, there had to be a better way than this!

At the top of the stairs, I checked the corridor. It was clear and quiet. Not good. That meant I was late for class! Ms. Lawler looked up when I entered the room and said, "Abby, hurry. We're about to start." While everyone watched me, I found my way to my group. Michelle, one of the *fearsome four*, was in this class. She looked at me and then quickly turned away. For sure, she'd report this to *the group*. Good thing it wasn't math class! I would have had to face Stephanie, the ringleader. Have to tell Eden at lunch that this plan might help me avoid *them*, but my teachers will become suspicious if I'm always late for class.

The bell rang for lunchtime! The cafeteria lunch line crawled along. I wasn't paying too much attention to the food I put on my tray. "Let's see," the lunch lady said when I pulled up to pay. "Two sandwiches, two milks. Extra hungry today, hon?"

"Oh, I only meant to get one of each. Sorry." My face heated up.

"That's okay. That'll be one sixty-five. I'll take these back," she said, removing the extras.

Eden looked up at me as I got close to his table. "So?"

Okay, here it was, the moment of truth. If I told him how bad it was, he'd think I didn't appreciate what he was doing to help me. "Pretty good. Only a few problems," I said.

"What? Tell me." He was anxious to hear.

"I got to the first class on time but was late for the second. I ran into the seventh-graders downstairs changing class."

"Uh-oh! I didn't think about that. But you didn't bump into any of *them*, did you?"

"No."

"So, part of it worked!"

I hated lying. "Yeah, part of it."

"Let's see how this afternoon goes. Then we can map out the rest of the week."

"Okay." When I looked at my tray, I realized that I had taken the wrong kind of sandwich.

"What's the matter?" Eden asked.

"Nothing important. I hate fish."

"Here, switch. I got slices of pizza."

"Are you sure?" I couldn't face a fish sandwich just then.

"No problem." We traded plates.

I was starved. My mouth was so busy I almost forgot to thank him. I nodded and smiled through a mouthful of pizza. He pointed to his fish sandwich, stuck his thumb up, and smiled back as he chewed.

✻ ✻ ✻

The afternoon was as bad as the morning. I rushed from one stairway to the other, huffing and puffing as I entered each classroom. Paying attention in class was not any easier either. I'd just tell Eden the experiment was working but I wouldn't do it. How would he find out? Except for social studies, his classes are in a totally different wing.

After school I sat across from Eden and heard myself lie to him once again.

"So, how did this afternoon go?" Eden sat forward in his chair.

"Better than this morning. Much better. I never

met one of them and got to class on time. Maybe I'm getting faster." I smiled.

"Great! Okay, let's plan the rest of the week out." He pulled the student handbook open to the building map. Several times as I sat there watching him, I opened my mouth to tell him the truth, but nothing came out. A half hour later, he had the whole week planned out. No way I could be honest now. I was in too deep.

"Thanks." I folded the sheets and put them into my pocket. "I guess I'll report to you at lunch tomorrow."

"Want to look at the math now?" Eden asked, hopeful.

"Okay. What did you cover today?"

"Integers. What about you?"

"Same thing. Want to check our work?"

"Yeah." I was glad we got away from thinking about his schedule for me.

Our heads fell over our textbooks, and we shared answers to the problems.

We were concentrating so hard neither one of us noticed the time. Soon the block of sunlight that traveled across the middle of the table slid off the side. It was time for me to go home.

"So, see you tomorrow at lunch, right?" Eden confirmed.

"Yeah. Save me a space."

"Abs, we're the only ones at the table. You'll have your choice of places to sit."

"I know. I just wanted to see if you were paying attention." It was fun to joke with Eden.

"Got it! Tomorrow, let's work on social studies."

I waved and walked down the ramp and across the lawn to the back door of our house. Once I flicked the switch, the kitchen came alive with light. If I came into the house when it was dark, I turned the lights on quickly. Usually, I flipped on lights in every room from the back to the front of the house before I went upstairs to my bedroom. Then even if I had no reason to use it, I turned on my computer. Its humming kept me company. Who would ever think a computer could act like a friend?

About a half hour later, the back door rattled and opened followed by the rustling of plastic bags. "Abby! Come help me," my mother yelled up to me.

I rushed down to the kitchen and scooped up bags of groceries from the back porch. "Put those frozen things in the freezer," my mother said. "Why are all the lights on?"

"It was dark when I came in. It feels weird when there's no light on in the house," I said, placing bags of frozen vegetables and cardboard containers into the freezer.

"Oh, Abby, when will you get over that?" my mother complained.

"When I grow up, I guess."

"Abby, you're twelve. Isn't it about time to stop being afraid of the dark?"

I closed my ears and pointed my brain at placing cans of soup in the cupboard, one on top of the other with the labels showing out. I liked things to be in order. They made more sense that way.

"Now what are you two arguing about?" my father said as he closed the back door.

"Not arguing, David. I'm just suggesting to Abby that it's probably time to stop being afraid of the dark," my mother said.

"Some people never get over being afraid of the dark, Carol. As a result, they tend to be very careful when they are out at night, which is a good thing."

"Well, I think our role as parents is to help her deal with these childish ideas instead of letting them control her life."

"I think we should focus more on Abby's strengths instead of pointing out her weaknesses."

"Well, if you think you can do better, go ahead." The kitchen got dead quiet. My mother turned back to the grocery bags. Whatever was inside them got slammed onto the counter one by one. Bang, bang, bang, bang!

"It's not that I think I can do better. It's just …" He yanked his tie from his shirt collar. "Never mind. I'm going to change."

He faded into the hallway, mumbling to himself.

"Honestly, Abby, I wish you wouldn't upset your father like that. He's had a hard day at work."

"Me upset him! I didn't say a word."

"No, but you always disagree with me, and that upsets him." She took the empty grocery bag folded it on the counter and banged her hand against the edges as she talked.

I turned toward her. Now I was angry. "Mom, I did not disagree with you."

"I just wish that you would try harder to deal with some of the stuff that goes on in your life instead of waiting for us to tell you what to do."

My insides were boiling up. I knew if I said anything else, there would be another outburst from her. I grabbed the plastic bags from the counter, folded them carefully, and placed them under the sink. "Is there anything else you want me to do?"

"Yes, scrape those carrots and put them into the steamer with enough water. Then set the table." She kept her back to me when she said it.

Chapter 6

Monday, on my way to lunch, I dodged kids in the school corridor. Bodies bumped and elbowed me from all directions, but suddenly, I felt four of them close me off from the others. I slowed down, and they did too. No matter what I did, they matched me. It was the pack!

"So, look who's finally decided to join us for a little talk. It's dumb Abby." With that, Stephanie, the blonde leader, pushed hard enough against my backpack to send me flying forward against the other three girls in the pack. My feet tripped over each other, and I fell on my knees. The four of them stopped walking and circled me.

"Gee, what just happened, Abby?" Karen, the one with long, dark hair, said. "Did someone knock you down?"

"Seems like she fell on her own. Let's help her up," Stephanie said in that singsong way she had. Three of the four girls bent down to lift me up, and before

I knew it, they shoved me into the nearby stairwell. When the door clicked shut behind us, I panicked. I held my books close to my chest, hoping they would cover the sound of my heart beating like crazy. If only someone would come through that door right now. Someone, anyone, just to stop them. They wouldn't do this if anyone saw them.

"Seems like Miss Abby here doesn't like to share with kids in her own classes," Stephanie said. "She has to go do a social studies project with dork Eden. I think that's kind of selfish, guys, don't you? Can't wait to see the project these two come up with."

"Yeah, probably twice as dumb as if they worked alone," Jen commented. She jerked her head back, and her blonde curls fell over her shoulder.

I kept quiet as I looked up at them. Stephanie grabbed my elbow and pulled me to the side of the landing.

"Maybe she thinks she's better than us," she said. "Well, we know different. So, what's your big idea, Abby? What's your topic? Maybe, like, 'Here's where Egypt is.'"

Three of them laughed. One kind of stood back from them, looking at me and then up and down the stairwell. Her face was all crunched up like she was afraid. She was in language arts with me, but I couldn't remember her name. My brain wasn't working right just now.

"Hey, yeah, maybe something like 'Egypt is a foreign country,'" Karen, the brown-haired one, said. Three of them laughed again.

"Hey, Abby, do you even know how to spell Egypt?" Jen said. Their laughter bounced off the metal stairs.

Stephanie put her hand against the wall and leaned over me. "Whatever it is, pea brain, we'll be around to see it. You know, so you can show us how smart you *aren't*." She said the last word loud, right in my ear. As she turned to leave, she shoved me into the wall so hard that my books fell to the floor. When I bent to pick them up, she jammed her knee hard into my ribs. I lost my breath and crouched down, folding my arms around myself to protect my side and my head.

"C'mon, guys. Why are we wasting our time on this pathetic thing?" Stephanie said. "She doesn't even defend herself." They opened the door and started to leave but the one in my English class held back and looked down at me. I raised my eyes and saw something in her eyes that was different from the other three, something soft. I swear she was going to say something until one of the other three shouted, "Michelle, come on!" The door shut behind her.

Once the door clicked shut, I knelt in a heap,

trying to catch my breath. Suddenly, the door on the upper landing opened, and two girls rushed down the stairs. I stayed bent over my books and pretended to look for something. The girls ignored me and passed through the doorway into the hall. Finally, I was alone. I wanted to curl up and cry. Not here, though. Other kids could have seen me. Word would spread like a wildfire that I was a crybaby.

Very slowly, I inched my side up the wall a little at a time and then took a deep breath and let it out, careful. Every move I made sent sharp pains into my side, but I managed to pick up my books. Walking was a little strange at first, but once I was in the corridor, my legs felt stronger. Now I was determined to see Eden before lunch period was over.

When I got to my locker, I turned the lock dial and let my backpack drop to the floor. Using my feet, I managed to lift it into my locker and throw the books on top. Without the weight, I moved much faster toward the cafeteria, but every now and then, a sharp pain hit my side. I placed my hand over my ribs and pressed gently. That helped.

Eden was still at his table, and no one was in the lunch line, so after I paid for an apple and some chips, I walked toward his table.

"Hey, Abs, are you excited that we can work together!"

"Yeah. I can't wait to get started. I put one hand on the table and the other on the back of the chair and then slipped my body onto the chair really slow.

"So, we can continue with what we started the other day," Eden said, pulling milk through his straw.

"Yeah, great!" I found that when I put both feet on the floor and rested my elbows on the table, my side did not hurt as much. But I had to keep myself from making any jerky moves.

"Hey, what do you think about mapping it out, kind of like an outline?" he asked.

"Sounds good." That was all I could squeak out.

Eden noticed me struggling to open the bag of chips, so he grabbed it, pulled the sides until it was open, and then handed it back.

"Thanks." I smiled back, hoping he wouldn't see anything in my face that would make him ask questions.

Sitting with Eden calmed me. Sometimes it felt like we had known each other for a long time. Kind of like Shelly and me. When I was with him, I felt … not safe exactly but more accepted, comfortable enough to be myself. It was a good feeling. A really, really good one.

✼ ✼ ✼

That night I sat at my computer desk, staring at the outline Eden and I had written after school. Coming up with ideas was no problem for us. The hard part would be finding information on the topics. We already divided our list of topics, and each of us tried to find as much information as we could on them. Next, we had to pick the one that we both liked best. A lot depended on which topic would give us the most information.

I looked at my choice. "How laws were made in Egypt." Right in the middle of the computer screen, the picture of Stephanie hitting me in the side popped up. Actually, my feelings hurt worse than my side. It wasn't fair that they got away with hurting me and that I couldn't think of a way to fight back. It was twice as unfair because I wasn't big enough to fight four of them! I shook Stephanie's face out of my brain and turned back to the outline. My insides were mushy with fear and hurt at the same time.

Shell, boy, do I wish you were here, I thought. When we were together out of school, the only thing we had to think about was how to have fun. Usually, she was the one who started things. I remember one time we were in the shopping mall with her mother. She told us to wait on the bench near a woman's store while she went in to buy something.

Shelly couldn't just sit and be quiet. She looked up at the mannequins in the shop window and pointed to one. "She looks like she just ate glue and it's making her cheeks stick to her teeth so she can't smile." Then she made her cheeks cave in like the mannequin's and looked at me. I laughed so hard. The more I laughed, the more she kept her cheeks pulled in. Then she pushed her lips out to look like fish lips to match the mannequin's, and she moved them like a fish does when it was breathing. I had to put my hands over my face and stamp my foot to keep from laughing too hard. But the thing that sent me over the edge was when she flapped her eyelids several times fast. I laughed so hard that people stared at me when they heard the strange sounds I was making.

When her mother came out of the store, she asked what we were laughing at. Shelly said, "Nothing," with that innocent look she could flash instantly. As we followed her mother through the mall, Shelly kept flapping her eyelids and making those fish lips at people. When her mother heard me laughing, she turned around. But Shelly instantly showed her normal, angelic face.

"Would you two walk on the other side of the walkway so people won't think you're with me?" she said, holding out her arm and flipping her hand like she was dismissing us. But I noticed as she turned her face away, the sides of her lips were curled up a little in a smile. Shelly kept her pantomime up all the way to the exit.

I couldn't remember the last time I laughed at something.

* * *

During the next day in language arts, we had to compare two characters in a short story we had just read in class. Ms. Lawler mixed up the groups every now and then so we wouldn't get too comfortable being with the same kids all the time.

When the pack cornered me the day before, the one who stood back like she was afraid of what they were doing was sitting across from me. Then I remembered Stephanie yelling her name—*Michelle*. I wondered if what they did bothered her. Maybe not. She was probably just afraid of getting caught. Or worse than that. Maybe she was afraid they might start picking on her if she left them. She didn't look at me. Then I wondered if she wanted to pretend I wasn't here. Too bad! Now she had to work with me!

"Now remember, folks, this is a group activity," Ms. Lawler said. "I'll be watching to see that everyone in the group participates. You are in new groups today, so I will give you some leeway for getting to know your group members. I still expect an effort on your part to make a connection and a contribution. You have twenty-five minutes before we come back to share."

As my group members turned back to share, Michelle still wouldn't look at me.

"Okay, let's see," Hadley, the third girl in the group, said. "We have to put down traits for each character and then see if they're alike in any way, right?"

"Yeah," Jerry, the only boy, said, "but we also need something from the story that proves they have that trait."

"Oh, right, like something they said or did," Hadley said. "How about if we pick traits first and then work in pairs to find things in the story that prove it," she suggested then looked at Michelle and me to agree.

I waited to see what Michelle would say. She turned her body away from me a little like she wanted to shut me out, and then she nodded her head. I did too.

"Okay, guys, ideas for characteristics," Hadley said. "I'll write them down."

Once we had a list, Hadley straightened herself up and announced, "I'll work with Jerry, and you two can work together."

There were two things I knew about Hadley. She liked Jerry, and she was bossy. Once again, I waited for Michelle to answer. Something sat on the edge of her tongue. Was she going to challenge Hadley? I wasn't going to give the pack any more ammunition to use against me, so I kept quiet. Finally, Michelle nodded. So, I did too.

Hadley moved her chair closer to Jerry, who quickly spread his elbows wide enough to prevent her from getting too close. I waited for Michelle to say something. She laid her copy of the short story on the table in front of her but left her chair where it was.

"So," she said, looking down at the paper, "which one do you want to do first?"

I hesitated, wondering if that was a trap. "Thoughtful?" I said like a question. That way I left it up to her to suggest another one.

She shrugged. I took that to mean she was okay with it. "When her grandmother was sick, she visited her and brought her some magazines." I looked over at her, waiting for some signal that she accepted what I said.

She nodded. "Yeah, and later she walked the dog for her neighbor who broke her arm." I wrote that down under my idea.

"So, that's two. Now ... trustworthy," Michelle said, still being careful not to look me in the eye.

"Well, when her parents went to the movies, she wouldn't let the other kids come into her house while they were gone," I said.

"Then later she wouldn't let one of the kids in her class copy her homework," Michelle said in response to my idea. I copied down what she said.

"Okay, now we have stubborn," she said.

I wondered how she would react if I suggested a different word. So far, we were doing okay here. I decided to push my luck, see how far I could go with her. "Maybe stubborn is the wrong word."

"What do you mean?" Surprise! She actually looked at me when she said this. I didn't see anything in her face that said she thought that was a stupid thing to say. More like she was interested. I kept going.

"It's more like she was determined. Like when she kept saying hi to the new girl in her class even when the girl wouldn't say it back. Our character just kept doing it until the new girl finally answered her. It's like stubborn is negative. You won't do something because you don't want to. Determined is positive. You keep doing something because it's a good thing to do." I waited, wondering if she would agree.

"Yeah, like she wasn't thinking about herself." There was a half-question in her voice. "Then there was the other time when she couldn't figure out the science experiment. It didn't make sense to her, so she did it at home again until she got it." At that moment it felt like some pressure between us broke.

I wrote our ideas down. When it was time to share with the other two, Michelle explained our decision to use *determined* instead of *stubborn*, and she gave me credit for it. Another surprise!

At the end of class, I was putting my papers into my binder. Michelle held back while the other kids left the room. She looked at me as if she wanted to say something. Instead she picked up her books and walked away.

I wondered what that meant. Would she still stick around in the background when the other three pounced on me?

Later that day after science class, I got my answer. Three of the four girls caught up to me in the hallway, and Michelle was with them. Stephanie grabbed the edge of my backpack and jerked it enough to send me off balance. I tripped and fell sideways.

"Hey, what happened, Abby? Your legs don't work right just like your brain."

From behind us a male voice said, "What's going

on?" Mr. Long, one of the science teachers, came up to us.

"Nothing, Mr. Long. Nothing's going on," Stephanie said, sounding all innocent. "We were just helping Abby. She tripped, and I was trying to keep her from falling."

Mr. Long looked really steady at Stephanie. "Oh, really? That's funny. From where I stood, it looked like you yanked her backpack, and that caused her to fall."

You probably could have knocked Stephanie over with a feather she was so surprised. But being Stephanie, she came to really fast and turned to Michelle and Karen. "Is that right, guys? Did I push Abby, or was I trying to help her?"

Karen burst open with a denial. "No way! Stephanie was trying to help her. I saw it."

"Michelle, what did you see?" Stephanie asked.

Michelle looked at me first. Her eyes said she was sorry, but her voice said, "She was trying to help her." She looked away from me.

"Well, get moving to your next class," Mr. Long said.

This was the first time someone saw something happen, and it was a teacher! I collected my books and stood up, then turned to follow the others.

"Hold on, Abby," Mr. Long said. "Is that what happened, what Stephanie said?"

"Whatever they said, Mr. Long." I looked away from him and adjusted my books.

"No, that's not the way it goes. Is there something going on here between you and these girls?"

Man, was I tempted to say something. All the times I had been shoved, tripped, embarrassed, and made to feel insignificant rushed to the front of my brain. Mr. Long could make it stop. Then I could come to school and not have to look over my shoulder every time I walked down a hallway. Not really! If I let Mr. Long fight this battle for me, they would find another way to get back at me, and it would be twice as bad. No way was I going to go through that.

"It's okay, Mr. Long, I'm okay. It was an accident. That's all."

He looked at me like he was searching for something. Finally, he said, "Okay, get along to class then."

I turned and headed down the almost empty hallway, moving away from safety, totally in the wrong direction.

✻ ✻ ✻

"So, did you find anything on your topic?" I asked Eden as I entered his kitchen.

"Speaking of finding things out," Eden said, "I

found out today that you lied to me." He looked up at me. The muscles in his face were as hard as stone.

I stood still. Shock waves shot through my body. I knew what he probably meant, but I did not want to admit it. "Lied? About what?"

"You told me the plan was working fine."

He knew something; I could tell. But what? I waited.

"If it's working, what were you doing in the upstairs corridor after science class today? You were supposed to go downstairs then." His face was a mask of anger.

"Uh, well … I forgot." If I let him see my eyes, he'd be able to tell I was lying. I was so bad at this.

"Come on, Abby. You didn't forget. I saw you two other times going down the upstairs corridor instead of the back way. What's going on?" Eden waited. His lips were a straight line across his face.

I slipped into the nearby chair and let my backpack fall to the floor. "Okay, you're right. I lied. I haven't been using the plan."

"Why not?" Eden sat back suddenly in his wheelchair and adjusted his cap. "I thought you said it worked fine. Did you even try it?"

"Yes, I did. I tried it the first day. Remember, I told you all about it at lunchtime? But—"

"But what?"

"I had to carry all my books for the morning with me, and that slowed me down. Then remember, I got caught in the seventh-grade corridor? I was late for class twice. By the time I got to class, I was so wiped out I didn't even know what we were doing. It kept me away from *them*. But I was wiped out, and that was only one day."

"Okay, I get all that," Eden said. "What I don't get is why you didn't tell me."

I talked to my hands. "I don't know. I guess I didn't want to complain. I didn't want to sound like a baby."

"It's more than that, isn't it, Abby?"

"Maybe." I turned my head to the side.

"So?"

"I … I didn't want to tell you because—"

"Come on, say it. Because?" Eden's voice softened. "Say it, Abby."

At this moment, I saw our friendship falling apart piece by piece. What would I do without Eden? He was my only friend, the only one willing to help me. With everything else going on, was I going to lose him too?

"Because I was afraid if I told you, I don't know. I guess I was afraid you'd be angry and I would lose you as a friend."

"Oh, man, am I glad to hear that."

I looked up at him and blinked. I was confused.

"I thought you were going to say you didn't want to bring it up because you felt sorry for me, didn't want to hurt my feelings. You know what I hate more than how much my body hurts and more than not being able to get around on my own? I hate the way people act like they feel sorry for me. They decide that if they talk about the things they can do in front of me that, somehow, it's gonna depress me. Or they don't tell me what they think about important stuff I say because they think it might hurt my feelings. So, they pretend to agree with everything I say just so they don't hurt my feelings."

I nodded my head and smiled.

"First thing, my number-one rule is my friends don't lie to each other. That's primo."

I nodded again.

"And my second thing is friends help each other out. So, if that plan didn't work, we have to come up with another one. Right?"

I looked up at him. "Yeah," I said. So, our friendship wasn't over! He wouldn't leave me on my own! I didn't think he would, but it was so nice to hear it. I almost cried I was so happy.

"Right now, we have to work on our social studies project. Besides, I need some time to think about another way to get these guys to leave you alone. Let me think about that, okay?"

Something in his face told me that he meant what he said. "Sorry, Eeds." (I don't know when I started to call him Eeds like his parents do, but it seemed to make him more like a best friend that just the kid next door.)

"Yeah, okay." He picked up a bag of chips from the counter. "Hey, I'm starved. Want some?" The old Eeds was back! I reached in the bag for some chips and took a deep breath.

Chapter 7

Except for having to live in a wheelchair, Eden never really acted like a kid with a sickness. Basically, he did whatever he could to work around it. So, I was not surprised one day when we were working on our project and he wanted a snack. His mother usually put one out for us, but she was busy with something for her business that day. Instead of bothering her, he turned to me and said, "Watch this." He picked up this silver, lightweight pole with a curved handle on one end. He squeezed a lever attached to the handle, and two curved pieces on the opposite end of the pole closed like a claw. Eden used this contraption to grab the knob of the kitchen cabinet and pull the door open. Then he squeezed the handle again to grab a bag of chips that he plopped on the table in front of us. Finally, he closed the cabinet door. "Cool, huh?" he said, placing the gadget on the table and ripping open the bag of chips. "I'm getting real good at this. I can even get myself a glass of milk." His eyes twinkled as he said this. Only Eden would think that going to that much trouble to get something to eat was cool. He never stopped amazing me.

It was Saturday, and we had two weeks left to figure out how to present the information for our project. "What do you think about making it into a game?" Eden asked.

"That might work. But we need to make it so that the information we found comes out somehow." It was important to me to share everything we had found out about our topic. Otherwise, it was, like, a waste of time.

"Yeah. We could do a question and answer thing."

"Okay, but don't forget we're going to be in the cafeteria with all the other sixth-graders. People will probably stop at our table for only a few minutes and then go to the next group. Whatever we do should be something that only takes a few minutes."

"Yeah, I get it. Something where they can get an answer fast. How about if we have the question about laws and regulations in our country now and ..." Eden bit into a chip and crunched away as he talked. "I'm not sure how we let them know about how it was in Egypt."

"Let's see. First, we have to make the questions easy enough for sixth-graders," I said. "If they can't answer questions about laws in our country, they won't even wait around to find out how it was in Egypt." I was amazed how easy it was for me to talk about my ideas with Eden.

"Got it. So, for instance, we might ask them to name one thing that keeps people from speeding through a town or city and causing accidents."

"Okay. So, do we give them a choice of answers and hope they give the correct one?" I was really getting into this. "Or maybe we have a bunch of possible correct answers, and if they give one of them, they get a bonus fact about laws in ancient Egypt."

Eden's face lit up. "Cool! So, we need questions that have several possible answers. That way they have a better chance of getting it right," he said. "Maybe we should start writing some questions and the possible answers that go with them and see how we do."

An hour later each of us had come up with a list of questions and possible answers for each. "Let's see how they work," Eden said.

"You first, then me," I said.

"Okay, so answer the first one I already said, the one about speeding and getting into accidents." I could tell by his face that he was excited.

"Let's see. One thing is stoplights."

"Yep, that's one of the answers. Now you."

"All right, if you run in the hallways at school, what could happen to you?"

"You could … get sent to the principal's office maybe." Eden wrinkled his forehead and waited for my response.

"Correct!" I yelled and gave him a thumbs-up.

We went back and forth like this until we had practiced all our questions. We both agreed that they were easy enough for most kids in our grade.

"You know, we could have, like, levels of questions from easy to challenging. Then when they answer one correctly, they move up to the next level."

Our project was coming together, and we were both excited about it. But what if our classmates didn't like it?

"What's up?" Eden asked. "What's on your mind?"

"I was just thinking. What if they don't like it? What if they think it's babyish or something?"

"You're kidding! How many sixth-graders do you know who don't like to play games? Besides, we're making it easy for them to play. They start easy and then gradually go up. They can stop at any point."

I had to agree with him. Eden had a way of getting rid of the wrinkles in things, like running your hand over your bedspread to even out the all the rough spots. He was beginning to rub off on me. I decided to stuff the worry deep inside myself, and whenever it tried to peek out, I would think of what he said.

Monday in math class, Mr. Gibson was at his usual spot in front of the room, explaining a way to solve a problem. When he finished, he said something that surprised me. "By the way, if any of you have a different way of doing this, I would like you to share it with us." Then he looked straight at me over his glasses. I heard a snicker from Stephanie, the pack leader. I looked down at my book and felt my neck and face get hot. As he was doing the problem on the board, I had already figured out a different way to do it. No way was I going to share it in front of *them* though.

As we were filing out of the room at the end of class, Mr. Gibson said to me, "Abby, hold back for a minute." When the room was empty, he pushed his glasses on top of his head and said, "I keep wondering why you hesitate to share what you know about solving problems. I can see now that you know how to do these problems in a different way. I hope I did not discourage you earlier, but I'm trying to encourage you to share your way with the others in the hope that they might explore other ways of doing problems.

Having you share how you do it would really help that along. You're the only one in this class so far who tries a different approach."

He thought that I could show the others a different way to do problems. This couldn't be real. "I like to fool around with the problems, Mr. Gibson. It's kind of fun to try to answer it a different way. It's nothing special."

"That's not true, Abby. You're in this particular class because you have strong math skills like the others. All of you had very good math scores in fifth grade, and your fifth-grade teachers recommended you. You are one of the best. Plus, I've noticed that when I give problems out in class, you are usually done far faster than the others, and your answers are always right."

"Really?" This warm feeling oozed into my chest. All this time I thought I was the dumb one in this class.

"Really. So, I'd like to see you share how you figure out different ways of coming up with answers with the others. Can you do that?"

This whole conversation was like a dream. None of it sounded real to me. "I don't know, Mr. Gibson. I'm okay with sharing my answers, but I'm not very good at explaining them in class."

"Do you do the problems your way first and come up with the right answers?" he asked.

"Yes." I was afraid to admit it.

"Think about this then. If you know something the others don't know, why should you be afraid of sharing it? If you get the right answer, how can they argue with you?"

I had to admit he was right about that. It was just that saying my ideas out loud in front of them, having them look at me and see how weird I looked was scary. But maybe that was because I thought I wasn't very good at math. "I'll think about it, Mr. Gibson."

"Here's another idea. Leave your solutions on my desk before class. I'll use it as an example for the others. That way, you wouldn't need to get up and explain it."

"I suppose that would be okay. As long as they don't know it's mine."

His hands were stuffed in his pants pockets. He looked at me for a moment as if he wanted to say something else, but he nodded instead. "Well, I can't promise to not tell them whose it is. If they press, I'll have to give your name."

"Okay," I said and waited for him to let me go.

"So that means you'll have to hand in your homework with both my way and your way. That's twice as much work for you."

"I always do them both ways so I won't lose any points." I looked back at him, wondering if he remembered what he had said about that.

He smiled, and then he reached up for his glasses and put them on the end of his nose. "Right. I did say you had to do it my way for credit. Okay then, you'll do it both ways. Maybe I should think about giving you extra credit for doing the problems twice. I'll have to consider that too." He looked over his glasses at me again. "See you tomorrow, Abby." He turned to a pile of papers on his desk. I left the room, carried by this cloud that had "Abby, Math Whiz" written across the side for all to see.

* * *

After school I raced up the ramp to Eden's back door. I was so excited about Mr. Gibson's talk with me that I wanted to share it with Eden. When I got close to the back door, the kitchen was dark. That was strange. I knocked anyway and waited. There was no sound coming from anywhere inside the house. I knew he planned to be there. For some reason, it seemed like something was wrong. I walked down the ramp and around to the front door. No one came when I rang the bell. Maybe Eden had a doctor's appointment that he forgot to tell me about. No! He always knew when they were because he hated to go so much. The idea that something was wrong kept nagging me. I crossed the yard to my back door and went in. My excitement over what Mr. Gibson had said to me faded. I was starting to worry about Eden.

At my computer I tried to concentrate, but my mind switched back and forth between what was on the screen and Eden's darkened house. My ears were tuned to outside noises for any sound that might tell me he was back home. The only thing I heard was my mother coming in the back door.

I came to the top of the stairs. "Hey, Mom, I'm here," I yelled to her so that she wouldn't be surprised.

"Abby! I thought you and Eden were going to work on your project."

"We were, but he's not home."

My mother came into the hallway to put her coat in the closet. "Oh! Did you know he wasn't going to be there?"

"No," I said.

"Well, something must have come up, and he couldn't get in touch with you. Did you check the answering machine?"

"Yeah, nothing on it. I know Eden. He would have left a note or something to let me know."

"Well, don't worry. I'm sure nothing's wrong." She walked back to the kitchen.

"Something *is* wrong. I know it!" I said into the empty air above the stairs.

Just then the phone rang. My mother's voice entered the hallway below me. "Oh, hello, Mrs. Gray. This is Carol, Abby's mom." My ears perked up. "I'm glad you called. Abby was very worried. Let me put her on. Abby, pick up the phone upstairs. It's Eden's mom."

I went into my parents' bedroom and picked up the extension. "Hello."

"Abby, this is Mrs. Gray. Eden wanted me to let you know why he is not home to work with you. He's in the hospital, Abby."

"Hospital! Is he all right?" My stomach flip-flopped.

"Yes, he is. It's a precaution. He started to come down with a cold yesterday, and by the time he came home from school this afternoon, he was having problems breathing. That happens every now and then. We have to be careful about it because of his condition."

"Oh," I said. I didn't know what else to say. "Is he still there? In the hospital, I mean?"

"Yes, he'll be there overnight so they can stabilize him. He might come home tomorrow or the day after. But he wanted you to know he'll do whatever he can to help you with the project even if he can't be there for the presentation."

What she said at the end did not sink in until later because I immediately said, "When he comes home, can I visit him?"

"As long as he's not on the respirator because then he couldn't talk to you very well. Why don't I leave a message for you on the back door before I leave for the hospital tomorrow? By then, I should know when he's coming home."

"That's good! Mrs. Gray, tell him I'm sorry he got sick. Tell him I'd like to come visit him."

"I will. That will perk him up. Thanks, Abby." The phone buzzed as I stood there holding it, staring into space. All I could think of then was Eden lying on a hospital bed, his mouth covered by the respirator mask to help him breathe. *What does that mean? I asked myself. Is he going to die? His mother didn't say that, but is that what it means?* Back in my room, I flopped on my bed and reached for one of my stuffed animals.

The picture of Eden lying quietly in a hospital bed didn't seem right. Even though he sat in a chair all day, he had piles of energy. He was always moving around, talking, and making jokes. His being sick was the part of him that I didn't think a lot about, mostly because he didn't make a big deal out of it. But if they had to do something to help him breathe, that was serious! What if he started to have trouble breathing when we were working together? I don't even know what I would do to help him. That scared me a little. I knew then that I had to ask him about it before it happened. Usually, there was someone with him no matter where he was—his mom at home and his para at school. Still, just in case, I needed to know.

Chapter 8

Eden did not come home the next day or the day after that. Whenever I thought about him not being able to breathe, I pulled air into my lungs. On Thursday, it finally hit me. I might have to present the project without him! My stomach tightened up.

Standing at my open locker, I was feeling lucky about not meeting up with the pack. It had been more than a week since they beat on me in the stairwell. But any hope I had that they were picking on someone else disappeared instantly when I turned and found all four of them facing me in a semicircle.

Big mouth Stephanie spoke first. "So, look who's here, guys. It's our favorite sixth-grader. How's the project coming, Abby? Now that mister flabby legs is out of circulation, who's gonna do your project for you?"

"Yeah, Abby," Karen's chimed in. "Now you won't have anyone to hide behind. Everyone will see how dumb you really are."

"I can't wait until Monday," Jen said. "Your table will be the first one I visit." Her voice sounded like she was challenging me.

Michelle, the one who was in my English class, stood back a little from the others like she had the last time, like she did every time. Her eyes sent a message that confused me. Was she apologizing? What good did that do me? Why didn't she open her mouth and tell them to back off?

"See you Monday, dumb Abby," Stephanie said. "It should be a real fun day for us."

With that, they headed in different directions. The funny thing was that they didn't hit me or knock my books out of my hands, which was strange. I held back a little before starting toward my math class. I made sure to stay way behind Stephanie.

✳ ✳ ✳

On Tuesday and Wednesday when I entered math class, Mr. Gibson looked up at me without saying anything. I guess he was hoping I had agreed to share my solutions. But I hadn't decided to do it until last night. When I was sure no one was looking, I slipped my papers on his desk before going to my seat. I saw him pick them up, read them, and smile. *Please don't look over at me*, I thought. *Good, he didn't.*

Toward the end of class, Mr. Gibson turned from the whiteboard, snapped shut the cap on his magic marker, and said, "By the way, I am going to start a new practice in this class. I will give extra credit to anyone who comes up with a different way to solve any type of problem that we work on. For instance, here is another solution to problem seven from last night's homework." He grabbed a paper from his desk, uncapped the marker, and turned back to the whiteboard. As his marker flew across the surface, I saw my solution on the whiteboard! That was so cool! "Do you see how this eliminates step two of my solution by factoring these four numbers together? It eliminates that step, replaces it with something faster, and comes up with the same answer as mine. It happens again here in step four." He stepped back and let the class consider what was on the board.

"Mr. Gibson," one of the students said, "we don't know as much math as you do. How can we come up with a different way of doing problems?"

"By looking at this whole process differently," he replied. "Once you learn how to follow a formula, try to find another way to solve problems that works but might be faster, more efficient."

"But Mr. Gibson, do you really expect a sixth-grader to come up with a different way of doing these problems?" another boy said.

"This was done by a sixth-grader." He held up my papers. From my seat I couldn't tell whether or not my name showed through the paper. I looked around, but I didn't see anyone whispering to anyone else. As far as I could tell, my secret was safe.

"That was done by a sixth-grader?" someone asked.

"Yes." Mr. Gibson crossed one arm over his chest, and with his free hand, he pulled on his earlobe several times. He did that whenever he was trying to make a point.

"Someone in this class came up with that?" another kid asked.

"I didn't say that," Mr. Gibson answered. "Don't forget. I have five groups of sixth-graders."

"Must be some kid from the smart group then," said one girl.

"In fact, it's someone in this class." Oh, no. He did what I had asked him not to do.

"Who is it, Mr. Gibson?" one kid asked. "At least give us a hint."

No, no, no. Please don't do it. "This was submitted by Abby."

"Hey, Abbie, cool," said one boy.

"Yeah, can we do math homework together," said one girl. I didn't know whether to take her seriously. I smiled and shrugged my shoulders.

"Anyway, folks, if any of you are interested, let me know. Of course, this means you have to do the problems twice, once my way and then your way."

"I'm pretty sure I won't be volunteering for that, Mr. Gibson," one boy said. "I hardly have time to do it your way."

"Just putting it out there, folks, for anyone interested. It's a way to earn extra credit."

The final bell pinged above us. Students slapped their binders shut and left the room, mumbling to one another. Some looked over at me and smiled. Except for Stephanie. She stared at me and bumped against my desk before leaving the room. Okay, there it is— threat number two.

"Well, Abby, we'll see what comes of it. Mind if I use these with my other classes?" he asked, holding up my papers.

"Sure, Mr. Gibson. At least I didn't have to explain it in front of them."

"We have to work on that, Abby."

Yeah, and the next thing you know, the pack will say that I'm the teacher's pet and Stephanie has one more reason to hate me. I nodded, but I didn't look at him.

* * *

After school but before going into my house, I plodded up the ramp to Eden's back door. The air was cool, almost cold, and the sun was fading. Summer was pretty far behind us now. The kitchen light was on. Eden's Mom came to the door with a wide smile.

"Abby! Eden's going to be awfully happy to see you. Come on in."

"I'm glad he's finally home," I said.

"So is he. One more day in the hospital, and he would have found a way out on his own. His bedroom is down this way."

Since Eden and I always did homework at his kitchen table, I had never been beyond the kitchen before this. Mrs. Gray guided me down a hallway toward the back of the house. "Eed's room is down here. That makes it easier for him to get around. Eeds, guess who's here?"

"Mom, if it's my therapist, I'm not decent."

"No, much better than that. It's Abby!"

"Hey, Abs, cool! Come on in!"

"Hi," I said, but my voice sounded weak because I was used to seeing Eden in a wheelchair. I was surprised when I entered his bedroom. Set in the middle of his room with four walls plastered with posters of

tos, there was a large bed like
l. Above it, a bar hung from a
ead. The back of the bed was
im, but he grabbed the bar to
as sitting up straight.
ir over here," he said, pointing

essed a button, and the back of
e could rest his back against it.
s mother asked. I noticed that
f the bed and didn't fuss around
ed to. He did everything okay
by himself.

"Yep. Hey, Abs, how's the project coming? Sorry I
wimped out on you. Are we all set?"

"Almost, just a few things to do." I didn't want him
worrying about it.

"Yeah. Well, we've got all the questions done,
right?"

"Right."

"So, all we need is a poster. Got any ideas about
what it should have on it? I could start to work on it
tomorrow while you're in school."

Things like this surprised me about Eden. I came
here to visit him because he was sick, and he acted like
it was just a regular day for us. It took me a minute to

get used to. "You're gonna work on it? You're supposed to be sick."

"Nah, just a little blip. I'm fine. Matter of fact, I'm probably going to get out of bed tomorrow. I think we might have some cardboard around here. If not, I'll ask my mom to get some at Staples. And some markers. Do we need different colors?"

"Uh, yeah, I think so." He was acting like nothing happened between now and the last time we worked together, like his being in the hospital was a little thing.

"Okay, let's figure out what we want it to say. Hand me that pad and pen from over there." He pointed to his desk.

Twenty minutes later we had sketched out the poster. We decided to print the questions on a sheet of cards that people put into plastic name tags. Since Eden's mom had a good printer at home, she could help him with that. My job was to print out all the facts about Egypt that would be the prize for answering correctly. We wanted to give out candy for a prize, but our teacher said learning something new should be the take-away from all the projects not something sweet which wasn't good for us anyway. That sounded like something our parents would say but we knew we had to cooperate or we might lose points from judges.

The one thing missing—the most important piece

for me anyway—was for me to know whether Eden would be there. How could I be at the project table without him? This was not good. Then the picture of Eden trying to catch his breath came into my head. I knew then that I would at least show up and be at the table, and if he couldn't be there, I had to try to make it work—for both of us. Being scared about it stayed with me. But the way he got past being in the hospital gave me some courage, but only a little.

The next day after school, Eden and I met again to finish everything up. Then we worked on the poster. Eden asked me to do the printing because his hand wasn't that steady. Across the top we wrote, "Would You Have Liked Living in Ancient Egypt?" Under that in smaller print, we wrote, "Learn How Our Laws Compare to Theirs—Play This Game." We made the word *game* fancy with different colors so it would stand out. That was Eden's idea.

He found pictures of Egyptian buildings and symbols on the internet for the bottom and sides of the poster. We also found symbols of things that were connected with laws in our society like street and highway signposts and a policeman and policewoman. These we pasted on cardboard. We glued a piece of folded cardboard to the back as a stand so they would stand upright. With the poster, the stand-ups, and the questions cards, our project looked pretty impressive. We'd find out how it would work on Monday.

Then Eden had this brilliant idea to try it out on our parents. The next day was Saturday. That was perfect. Since everything was at Eden's house, his mother suggested that I bring my parents over to their house, and we would set it up there.

✳ ✳ ✳

My mother wasn't crazy about the idea, but my father convinced her that she owed it to me to support this project. "Look, Carol, Abby and Eden have been working on this for almost two months. The least we can do is give them a little help by doing a dry run."

"But we don't know Eden or his parents. I've only talked to his mother once. It will be awkward."

"Well, don't you think this is the perfect opportunity to introduce ourselves," my father asked.

"I'm not sure." We were at supper. My mother looked down at her plate and fiddled with her silverware. Now I was getting angry. Wasn't she always telling me to get out and make friends? Now look at her trying to get out of meeting our neighbors!

"Whether you go or not, Carol, I will," My father's voice was pretty definite. "I am not going to let Abby down." With that, he folded his napkin and put it on the table. My mother looked at him and then at me.

"I guess this is important to you," she said.

"Yeah, it is." I looked right back at her.

"Well … all right, I'll go over for a little while. When are you going to do it?"

"Mrs. Gray said they're flexible, so it's up to you guys."

"Well, how about two o'clock?" she suggested. "That way I can get my laundry and housecleaning done."

"Cool! Thanks, guys. I don't know if Eden's going to be there on Monday, so it will help to practice with someone."

"How long do you think it will take?" my mother asked.

"That depends on how much you know about laws in our country, I guess." I wanted to see what she would say back to that.

Her forehead wrinkled. "I thought this was a project on Egypt," She started to eat.

"It is. We compared living in our society with living back then. We're showing how laws were made and enforced then and how we do it here."

"Pretty interesting stuff, Abby," said my father. "Whose idea was it?"

"Eden and I came up with it together. We think a lot alike. It's easy for me to talk to him."

"Well, I'm interested to see how you put this together," my father said. "You both have certainly put a lot of time into it." My father sipped his water.

"Yeah, I just hope it goes over okay." With my fork, I drilled a hole in my mashed potatoes.

"Why wouldn't it?" my father asked.

"I don't know. You never can tell." I piled some peas into the middle of my mashed potatoes.

"If you did all that work, your teachers will certainly see it," he said.

"Yeah, I guess." I had to be careful. I didn't want anything to slip out about the pack.

"Is there anything we should know about?" My father looked over at me.

This conversation was going in the wrong direction. "Huh? Oh, no. I'm a little nervous. That's all. I don't like to talk in front of people."

"But it will mostly be your classmates. Right?" my dad said.

If this kept going, I'd have to admit the real problem. "Yeah, I guess you're right, Dad." I shoveled some potatoes into my mouth and put on a happy face.

✳ ✳ ✳

Saturday, fingers of sunlight around the edges of the shade in my bedroom woke me up. I pushed my toes against the sheets and made two little hills at the end of my bed. I wish it was Tuesday, and this whole project thing was over. If Eden was going to be there, I'd feel better about it. He was the one who knew how to deal with people. He liked kidding around and making them laugh. But I'd rather be by myself reading a book.

Then there was my mother. I almost wished she wouldn't go over to the Grays'. *Will she say anything embarrassing? I thought. I hope not. Do I really have to go downstairs and look at her stony face first thing in the morning? Maybe I'll turn over, go back to sleep, and wake up at noontime. Nope, can't. Have to do some final things on my project.* I flipped my legs over the side of the bed and stuck my feet into my slippers.

A mixture of excitement and nerves was rumbling around inside my stomach as I went downstairs for breakfast. When I found my dad sitting alone, reading the paper at the kitchen counter, the knot in my neck loosened up.

"Hi, honey. So, this is the big day." He folded the newspaper and placed it on the counter. His eyes searched my face as he sipped his coffee.

"Yep, trial run. But if it doesn't work right, it's kind

of too late." I pushed myself up on my toes and slid onto the stool at the counter and then reached for a glass. My dad slid the orange juice container over to me.

"Well, you have today and tomorrow to work out any wrinkles. That should be enough time."

"Yeah, I guess." I lifted the container to the glass and watched that little hole form in the center of the liquid while the rest of it splashed up the sides of the glass. That always made me think of what it must look like inside a hurricane funnel. Once I stopped pouring, the hole rose to the top. The juice evened out and became still like the ocean did when a storm had passed. "Dad, can I ask you something?"

"Sure, honey."

"How come some kids seem to have a hard time fitting in? You know, being popular?"

"Hmm. Interesting question," my father said, resting his chin on his hand and looking down at his coffee mug. "Not sure I can answer that. Sometimes I think it's because they don't want to fit in. Other times I think it's because they're not interested in what most kids are interested in. If the kid being made fun of is smart, I think the kids who aren't very smart get jealous about how easy it is for smart kids to learn and get good grades, which teachers and parents like. I remember when I was your age, the kids I hung around with made fun of one kid in our class who was really smart. I didn't do it, but I heard the comments often enough. Then when I would try to defend him, my friends would call me names. I guess making fun of that kid made the others feel better somehow. I think they tried to convince themselves they had something better than the smart kid like being stronger or better at sports or just more normal, which they decided was the best thing to be."

"What about kids who aren't smart but don't fit in?"

"Ah, I think that's another ball of wax. It's almost like those kids don't have to do anything. They just become a target for someone who needs a target, someone to rough up. Another kid in our class came from a poor family. He didn't have any sports equipment like a glove or a bat and ball. He tried out for the team but didn't make it, but you could tell he liked baseball because he would sit at the edge of the ball field and watch the games. One of my friends made a point of calling him a loser every game he did that. Nothing I said would stop it. I always felt bad about that. Anyway, honey, why did you ask?

"Oh, nothing. Just wondering." I took the final sip of orange juice.

"Any problem at school about this?"

"Huh? Oh, no, Dad. Just thinking."

He looked at like he wanted to ask more about that, but at that moment, my mom stepped up into the kitchen from the basement stairs. She breathed heavily as she held onto the laundry basket and closed the door with her foot. She set the basket on the kitchen floor "You know, Abby, I think it's time you learned how to do laundry. Sometimes it seems like all I do is housework. I hardly get any time to relax."

In my view, that was her way of saying that she didn't want to go to our neighbor's house this afternoon. "Sure, I could help. You never asked me before."

That must have surprised her because she shot a look at me that said she was trying to figure out if I was being, like, rude. "Well, I think the time has come."

"But not today, Carol," my father said. "Today, Abby needs to focus on her project."

"Speaking of that," I piped in, "I have to go up and print off some stuff for this afternoon." Before I left the kitchen, I turned to my dad and said, "Thanks, Dad."

"You're welcome, honey."

"Laundry classes start next weekend then," my mother said over her coffee.

"Got it, Mom." I gave her a thumbs-up. "I'll be there." As I walked away, I wondered what her answer would have been about fitting in.

Chapter 9

Watching my mother get ready to go over to the Grays' house was like watching someone leaving home for prison. Fifteen minutes before we had to leave, she sprayed and cleaned the kitchen counter, moving every article and then pushing each one back. Then she pulled the vacuum out of the closet and did a quick run over the kitchen, the dining room, and living room.

"Carol, we're going to their house, not having them over. Why are you doing this now?"

"I won't have time later, and I want this done."

I couldn't watch this anymore. "I'm going over to make sure everything's ready," I said and headed out the door.

Eden had set our project up on the dining room table. We had chosen a bright-colored yellow poster board that made the black print and the pictures really stand out. I had to admit, I did a great job on printing the poster. Mrs. Gray had suggested that I draw lines before I printed the words, and it made a big difference. No slanted words. Along with the stand-up figures of people and symbols of law and the colored question cards, the whole thing looked like a big birthday present.

"Hey, Abs, I think kids will come to our table first just because it's the brightest."

"Yeah, everything looks great! Here are the bonus fact cards." I laid the pile of cards on the table.

"Abs, you haven't met my father yet. Dad, this is Abby, the brains behind this project. She's the one with all the good ideas."

Eden's dad put his hand out. "Nice to finally meet you, Abby." I liked his friendly face.

"Thanks, Mr. Gray. My parents are on their way over."

"Let's wait till they get here before we give you the directions," Eden said to his parents.

Just then the doorbell rang, and Mr. Gray went to the door. I could hear him introducing himself. I held my breath, listening for some ridiculous thing my mother might say.

Mrs. Gray came out of the kitchen and joined her husband at the front door. "Hi, I'm Pam."

"Nice to finally meet you both," my father said. He was good at stuff like that.

My mother carried a homemade frosted cake on a plate. Where had that come from? "I apologize for not bringing this over sooner. Welcome to the neighborhood. It's nice to finally meet you face-to-face."

"How nice of you to take the time," Eden's mom said. She took the plate, put her hand on my mother's shoulder, and guided her into the dining room. "Isn't it surprising how busy we get? Ed and I can't believe we've been here for more than two months already. Come on in." I could tell from my mother's face that she felt pretty comfortable right away.

"Mom, Dad," I said when my parents approached us, "this is Eden."

"Thanks for coming to help us," Eden said, extending his hand to my dad, who gave it a strong shake.

"Our pleasure, young man." My mom smiled but said nothing.

"So, this looks very impressive, honey," my dad said, looking at me. "What would you like us to do?"

I looked at Eden to do the intro. "Okay, here's how it works," Eden said. Our parents gathered around us. "We have three sets of cards here with questions on them about laws in our country. You start with an easy question, and we have a bunch of possible answers, so all you have to do is give one of them. If you get the answer right, we give you a bonus point fact about laws in Egypt. Don't worry. We made the questions *easy*," he said, smiling wildly at his mom. She gave him a thumbs-up. "Oh, by the way, if you don't get the answer to the question, we give the opposition a chance to answer it, and they get a bonus point fact. Since there are two couples here, maybe you guys can form two teams. I'm adjusting these directions as I go along, but it sounds like a good idea. What do you think, Abs?"

"Yeah, I like it."

"Which team wants to go first?" Eden would make a good game show host.

"I guess it makes sense for us to work together," my father said, putting his hand around my mother's waist. "We'll take the plunge."

"Okay, here we go." Eden picked up a card. "What could happen to someone who lets the meter run out on their parking space?"

My dad looked at my mom and said, "He or she could get a parking ticket."

"Correct!" Eden shouted. "And for your bonus point, you get an interesting fact about Egyptian law that will be given by my brilliant colleague." He stretched his arm out toward me.

"In Egypt, according to the concept of Ma'at," I read, "everyone except for slaves was viewed as equal under the law."

"That's interesting," my dad said.

"Okay, now you guys," Eden said, looking at his parents. "I'll give you the easiest one we have. Okay, in order to legally drive a car, what must a person do?"

Eden's parents turned their heads toward each other and spoke quietly, and then his mother said, "Have the keys."

"No, c'mon, Mom. Be serious."

"Okay, Eeds, sorry. Get a license."

"Great! Your bonus prize fact from Miss Abs."

"In Egypt, when someone was found guilty of a crime, that person's whole family was punished as well."

We went back and forth like that a few more times, moving up to the harder questions. My parents tied with Eden's parents. They laughed about that. Then when Eden and I declared the game a draw, Mrs. Gray invited my parents to have coffee, and she brought out my mother's cake.

Eden and I talked about how positive we felt about our project. We decided that if someone couldn't answer more than two questions, we would give them a bonus fact just for playing. That was the point of the project after all—to share information about Egypt. The game was a way to do that. While our parents sat in the living room and talked, Eden and I went to the kitchen to write out a few more easy-level questions.

"So, Abs, since I'm not absolutely sure I can go to school on Monday, I guess you should take all the stuff with you just in case," Eden said.

"Okay. I'm pretty sure my dad can give me a ride in on Monday. Boy, I sure hope you're there. You really make it work."

"I'm gonna do my best to be in school. If I still have trouble breathing though, my mom probably won't let me go."

I crossed my fingers. "Here's hoping."

"Yeah," Eden said, "but you don't need me to make this work. You're the one who designed it and found most of the information about Egypt."

"That's not what I'm worried about."

"Oh, you mean *them?*"

I nodded.

"Look, Abs, you know they're losers. What do you think they can do in a public place like that? I mean, the whole school will see them."

"They can embarrass me. That's what."

"How can they do that when they have to be with their own projects?"

I hadn't thought about that. "I don't know. They said they would be there first thing. Knowing them, they'll find a way to do something." I felt gloomy and afraid just talking about it. My chest heaved as I tried to calm down.

"Okay, Abs, I'm gonna really rest tomorrow so I can be there on Monday."

"You think we should stay there all day?"

"Well, if I'm there, it won't be a problem because we can take turns to go to the bathroom and get our lunch."

"What if you can't be there?" A feeling of helplessness washed over me.

"Don't worry about it. I'll be there."

I wanted to believe that. Knowing my luck, something would prevent that from happening. I nodded my head but said nothing.

Eden must have sensed that I was not sure. "Do you think I'm gonna let them do anything to this project? It's mine as much as yours. This is personal now." Eden had a way of making you believe what he said. It must have been the way he said it more than what he said.

✻ ✻ ✻

On Monday morning a line of cars formed a semicircle around the front of the school. Kids pulled posters and bags of stuff from the back seat of their parents' cars and SUVs. Project day!

"Got everything, honey?" my dad asked. "Do you want me to park in the lot and help you?"

I pulled my backpack over my shoulders until it sat on my back. We had put all the cards and the stand-up figures in a bag with handles, and the poster was covered with a sizeable trash bag that I held by the neck to keep it off the ground. "I think I have it, Dad. Thanks."

"Good luck, honey."

"Thanks." I joined the line of kids carrying projects through one of the front doors of the building. The assistant principal directed us to leave our projects in the cafeteria until after homeroom exercises. Eden had told me to guard the materials. I had to think of a way I could do that until it was time to come back and set up. I had stuck orange paper dots on my bags so that I would recognize them without anyone else knowing whose they were. Before finding a place to hide my materials, I looked around the cafeteria to see if any of *them* were watching me. From where I stood, I couldn't see any of them in the room. I stuck my bags behind a big machine that kept milk cool. The only way you could see it was to put your head close to the wall. Then I found our table at the end of a row close to the stage. A wide space for people to pass by separated our table from the edge of the stage. Since a lot of people would be walking back and forth there, it would probably be risky for the pack to do anything because they could be seen. I shook off some of my worry. Maybe this would work out okay after all.

At nine o'clock after attendance and the pledge were over, all the sixth-graders filed back downstairs to the cafeteria. I searched the room for Eden. There was no sign of him. Then I realized that in his wheelchair, I wouldn't be able to see him in this crowd anyway.

A hum hung over the cafeteria. I guess everyone was excited. Once I pulled the materials from behind the milk cooler, I headed for our table. It took me about ten minutes to put everything out.

All put together, it looked really cool with our bright-yellow poster and stand-up figures of lawmakers from Egypt's past and the United States in the present time. There were packets with questions on them. I also laid out the information packet that listed the resources we used for our questions—all from sources, not from Google. In addition to a two-page introduction explaining what our project was about, we had a five-page list of each fact we found on Egypt, and underneath it, we cited the title and author of the resource we had used for the answer, both online and offline articles. Our teacher said it was enough to just list all the resources, but Eden and I decided to label the resource for each fact. For Eden and me, the important thing wasn't as much how our project looked as much as what the visitors to our project could learn from our research. We had spent most of our time looking up information so that we would be comfortable that what we said was accurate.

Even though our teacher said we could take a quick walk around to see the other projects before the older kids came through, there was no way I was going to leave our table. Even if *they* did show up to bug me, I wasn't going to let them touch anything. Of course, I had no idea what I would do if they did make a move to damage something. Oh man, what *was* I going to do?

I didn't have to wait long to find out. Ten minutes after we all finished setting up, one of our teachers gave the signal to start our tour of the other projects. I planted myself at my table and waited. Sure enough, Stephanie and Karen appeared at the edge of my table.

"Well, look at this, a game. How cute!" Stephanie said. "What do you say, Karen? Should we play?"

"I don't know, Steph. Are we smart enough?" she said, rolling her eyes at Stephanie.

"So, come on. Give us the dumb directions," Stephanie demanded, batting her eyelashes.

I took a deep breath. "You answer one of the questions about laws in our country, and if you are correct, you learn a fact about laws in Egypt as your prize." I prayed they would say it was too babyish and leave, but they didn't.

"Go ahead. Ask us a stupid question," Stephanie said, her face all pointy with a challenge.

Maybe because I had gotten some good feedback from kids in my math class about the problem solution, but I had this sudden urge to be brave. I picked up a card from the hardest pile. I'd prove how smart she wasn't. "When someone is charged with a crime in our country, the police read a statement to the person that explains their rights. What is that statement called?"

Stephanie looked at Karen, who shrugged, and then she turned back at me. "What kind of a stupid question is that? Who cares anyway?" Stephanie said.

She was angry. *What a dumb thing for me to do. Here it comes. One of them will say something loud enough for everyone to hear.* I waited.

"Miranda rights," a boy said over my shoulder. I turned and saw one of the kids from our social studies class. "That's right in our social studies book."

It was perfect that he was there at that moment. You'd think I had *planted* him to answer the question.

"Right! Okay, your prize is a fact about Egyptian laws." I picked up my facts sheet and read a fact to him. "Before the Greeks imposed Roman laws on Egypt, the king was the person who made laws and was the supreme judge."

"Man, that's cool, Abby. Can I try another one?"

Stephanie and Karen looked at each other and then back at me. Stephanie spent a long minute looking at everything on the table before she looked me right in the eye. Without saying anything, she had gotten her message across. She would try to come back when I wasn't at the table and wreck some things. Then she and Karen turned and left. Who knows what they would do now? Why didn't I give her an easy question? That could mean trouble, big trouble.

"Do you want easy or hard?" I asked as I watched the two pack members walk away.

"You pick," he said as he turned to one of the sixth-graders passing by. "Hey, Carlos, come on over and play this game with me." About five minutes later, a crowd of kids stood in a semicircle at my table, playing the game. I managed to keep it going.

At 9:45, the hall started to fill up with kids from seventh-grade. Still no Eden. For at least forty minutes straight, I had a nonstop stream of kids at my table. Same thing happened when eighth-graders came through at 10:15. A few of the questions stumped the kids, but they laughed it off.

When the lunch bell rang, kids immediately headed to the front of the cafeteria to pick up their lunches. Since we were using the gym, all classes headed to their rooms to eat. After a while, I was alone with my project.

Except for dishes clashing and the lunch ladies talking in the kitchen, the cafeteria was quiet. I wondered if I could get away with staying in the cafeteria alone. It was the only way to be sure nothing happened to our project. I reached into my backpack for the breakfast bar and bottle of water I had brought with me. About ten minutes after the cafeteria became quiet, the door opened, and in walked Ms. Rodriguez, the assistant principal.

"Abby, we just got a call from your homeroom. What are you doing here?"

"I need to make a few last-minute changes before the judges come around."

"Abby, you can't be here by yourself."

"Please, Ms. Rodriguez. Couldn't I stay with my project a little while?"

"I'm sorry, Abby. Your project was supposed to be finished by the time you set it up this morning. It would give you an advantage over the other students to let you stay. Besides, you can't be here without a teacher."

I'll bet one of them will ask to go to the bathroom during lunch and sneak down here to steal or wreck something. But if I explained that to her, she would want to know the whole story. "Okay," I said. I looked at the table with all the question packs on it and wondered if they would be there when I returned. I was about to grab some of them and put them into my pocket when she said, "Come on. Let's get you back up to your class." I shoved the information packet into a bag and followed her out of the cafeteria. Walking away was like leaving a favorite pet in danger.

I sat in homeroom, worrying my head off. Finally, the chime signaling the end of lunch rang! Our room bustled with activity as kids lifted lunch trays or dropped plastic sandwich bags into the nearest wastebasket. We moved into the hallway packed with sixth-graders walking toward the stairway.

In the cafeteria, I searched furiously for our yellow poster. It was still standing. If the pack had not done anything during lunchtime, they could do it now on the way to their table. Why didn't I hide the question cards? Stephanie's and Karen's heads bobbed in front of me half way up the aisle leading to my table. They were getting close to our project, but the aisle was totally jammed with kids. I would never get there before them. I scooted back to the end of the tables and went up the next aisle to head them off. From where I stood, I saw Stephanie and Karen look over their shoulders as if checking to see who was watching them. Then they looked down at my table. I'd never get there in time. All they had to do was each grab a set of cards and put them into their pockets. I pushed furiously against sixth-grade bodies, but things came to dead stop when one kid pulled a box into the center of the aisle to take things out of it.

I pushed against the kid in front of me.

"Hey, Abby, what's the big rush?" he said.

"Stop pushing. I can't get where I'm going any faster," another kid yelled over his shoulder at me.

No way was I going to get there in time. They were at the project, and I couldn't move. Suddenly, they lifted their heads and turned around. I wasn't tall enough to tell what was going on, but it looked like someone had said something to them. I wondered who. I thought my heart would jump out of my chest it was beating so fast. It was already too late. The damage was done. All of the work on our project wasted! Finally, the kid with the box shoved it aside, and the aisle opened up. I rushed around to the table.

Eden was bent down, reaching for a pile of our question cards that were spread all over the floor.

"Abs, I made it!" he said, sitting back in his chair.

"Did you see them? They were standing right in front of the table. I thought for sure they would do something." My chest heaved in and out as I tried to catch my breath.

"They almost did! I came up behind them just as they were about to stash a bunch of cards into their pockets. I told them if they did that, I would start yelling bloody murder, and then the whole sixth grade would know what cheats they were. They dropped the cards like they were on fire and left."

"Boy, am I glad to see you," I said. "I thought you were out for the day."

"I almost was, but I convinced my mom that I felt fine. And I wanted to be here for the judges. I got here during lunch, and my para brought me in to see all the projects. It was nice having the whole place to myself. How did this morning go?"

"It was fine, I guess. The kids seemed to like the game. But without you, I had to keep the whole thing going. Right now, I'm pretty tired."

"You can relax. I'll do the judges."

Having Eden at the table lifted a huge weight off my shoulders. I plopped onto the folding chair by the table and fell into a spell; the sounds of excitement in the hall lulled me almost to sleep.

About ten minutes later, the judges started to visit each table. Two of them were from seventh- and eighth-grade social studies, and there was also a science, an english, and a math teacher from sixth grade. When they got to our table, my stomach tightened a little, but I settled down when I remembered that Eden said he would take care of the judges.

"So, tell us about your project and why you designed it the way you did," the seventh-grade social studies teacher said.

"Well, we wanted to compare laws from today with laws in ancient Egypt to kind of show how different it was back then from what we're used to," Eden explained. "For example, when someone in our country is arrested for a crime, many people, including policemen, lawyers, and judges, look at the crime and decide the person's innocence or guilt. In ancient Egypt, only one person did all that, the king. We designed it as a game because we thought that kids in our grade would rather play a game than read or listen to a lot of facts."

The math teacher looked at the card taped to the table that gave the name of the project and our names. "So, this is a joint project. Why don't you explain how it works?" The seventh-grade social studies teacher looked through our packet.

"Sure," Eden said, pressing the lever on his chair to

get closer to the table. "Okay, we have cards here with questions on them about laws in our country in the present time. They go from easy to hard." He touched each of the three piles. "If you are able to answer one of the questions on our laws, your prize is to hear a fact about how laws worked in ancient Egypt."

"Let's give it a try," one judge said.

"It works best if you work on teams, so how about if you have one social studies teacher on each team." Eden talked to these teachers like he was an adult. They moved themselves into two groups, and he pulled a card off the easy pile. "Oh, by the way, if one team can't answer, the other team gets a chance to try. Ready?"

"All set," they said.

Eden asked the first question, which the first team answered correctly. "For your prize, my colleague will give you a fact about law in ancient Egypt. Abby."

I noticed that the two social studies teachers looked through the information packet as the others answered questions. Once they went through a few rounds of the game, they wrote things on their clipboards, thanked us, and moved on.

"What do you think, Abs? How did we do?"

"Who knows? You did a great job of explaining it though," I said.

Once the judges finished, they left the cafeteria,

and the teachers told us to pack up our projects while we waited for the announcement of prizes. What a day! My head was in a fog. I exhaled, glad that it was finally over. All the kids left their packed materials on tables set up at the back of the cafeteria. All the kids sat on the cafeteria floor. I knelt at the end of a row with Eden's chair parked beside me.

The door to the cafeteria opened and the three sixth-grade judges walked to the long table in front of us. The seventh- and eighth-grade teachers must have had to go back to their classes. Our teachers raised their hands, and the room got quiet.

"Before we announce the prizes, we want to mention how impressed we were with all the projects," the math teacher said. "They showed a lot of work and a lot of thought. There are three prizes. Each judge rated each project on a scale of one to ten in the following three areas: the originality of the project design, presentation of information, and quality of the information. All the votes were added up, and the projects with the highest scores in all three areas are the winners of first, second, and third prizes. So, we will announce the prizes in reverse order starting with third prize."

The science teacher came forward. "The winner of third prize is … 'Egyptian Clothes for Women' by Andrea Compton and Maryellen Swift."

Students clapped and hooted while the two girls walked up to get their prize.

"Second prize is ... 'Farming in Ancient Egypt' by Jamie Stolz."

Once again, loud clapping and whistles sounded, and this time people were chanting, "Ja-mie, Ja-mie." He rushed up to get his certificate.

The language arts teacher now came to the center. By this time, I was ready to lie down and fall asleep. My brain was fried. "And now the prize for the project that got the most votes in all three areas. 'Law in Ancient Egypt' by Abby Wexler and Eden Gray."

I wasn't quite sure what had just happened, but suddenly Eden was hitting me on the back while all the other kids were clapping and hooting wildly. "Abs, Abs, we won! We won!" A knot formed in the back of my throat. "Come on, come on." The cafeteria filled with applause and whistles as I got to my feet and walked beside Eden's chair to the front of the hall. It was so strange to be in front of the room, looking at the sea of faces that smiled and clapped and hollered for us. I recognized most of the kids who cheered for us because they had come to our table and played the game. It was like a dream, a really nice dream. If all my dreams could be this good, I would never wake up.

Chapter 10

"Honey, are you serious? You won?" My dad stood in the middle of the kitchen with his hands stretched out.

"First prize," I said. "We won first prize."

"That's spectacular! Carol, isn't that great?" he said, looking over at my mother.

"Yes, that's really something!" She opened the refrigerator door. "Any suggestions for supper?" she asked.

Why am I not surprised? Anything like a compliment from her would amaze me. "The judges gave Eden and me the highest number of points in all three areas." She wasn't going to squash my big moment. "Here's the certificate." I handed it to my father.

He held it in his hand, and I saw a look cross his face. "I'm so proud of you, honey." He put his arm around my shoulders and squeezed hard. "Really proud. Not surprised, however." He bent his face toward me. "You and Eden, what a pair! Sounds like you have a good friend there."

"Yeah, I do." He was right. I never heard it said out loud before, but Eden was a good friend. Actually, my new, close, best friend. Shelly would now be my far, best friend … forever.

My mother stood at the sink pushing a sponge around the edges. She had not said anything else. Looking at the back of her head, I could almost hear the thoughts running around inside there, probably bumping into one another. I wonder if she will let anything out.

"I think this deserves a celebration. What do you think, Carol? Why don't we go out for supper?"

My mother immediately yanked open the refrigerator door. "I had planned a meal for tonight and need to use the meat, or it will spoil. Let's just have supper here. Abby got a certificate. That is her prize for winning."

She pulled a bag of something frozen out of the freezer, closed the door, and turned toward us. I saw this program on the Discovery channel once about a building imploding. Instead of blowing out like in an explosion, the whole thing caved in. That was how I felt.

"Are you kidding? This isn't just a case of getting

any prize," my father said. His voice had this energy I never heard before. "She and Eden won first prize for their project. That means the teachers judged them to have done the best job out of …" He looked down at me and asked, "How many kids in sixth grade?"

"I think around four hundred."

"Did you hear that, Carol? They did the best work out of four hundred others? As far as I'm concerned, that's pretty outstanding and deserves to be recognized in a special way by us."

My mother turned back to wipe the counter with a wet sponge. "Fine, if that's the way you think, you two go ahead. But I'm not going."

"Carol, I can't believe it." My father dropped his hand from my shoulder and put it on his hips. "Why can't you just let things from your mother go? They have nothing to do with this." My certificate flapped around in the air as he made jerky motions with his other hand. I had no idea what he was talking about. His voice was low, and his face was getting red.

My mother spun around in a split second. "What does that mean?" she demanded.

"That means that how your mother dealt with you has nothing to do with Abby. You shouldn't treat her the same way your mother treated you. It's not fair to her."

Okay, now I was totally confused. What did that mean?

"How my mother treated me has nothing to do with this." My mother's face became firm like a statue.

"It has everything to do with this, and you know it." My father jammed his finger against the kitchen counter when he said, "You know it." Now they stood face-to-face. I don't think either one of them remembered that I was in the room. This was the first time I had ever heard them argue in front of me. My mind raced. I tried to think of things to say that would stop them, but nothing came out of my mouth. I even thought of leaving the room, but something kept me there.

"That's rich coming from you," my mother answered. After each remark, my parents inched toward each other as if the closer they moved, the more their words would sting. "My mother never treated me the way your father treated you."

My father's head made this quick, backward movement as if something just hit him between the eyes. He stepped back. "At least I don't take it out on my daughter." His voice was low and even. "Now are you coming out with us or not?" he asked.

My mother straightened up and put one hand on

her hip. "No, I'm not," she said, looking directly into his face.

My father stood still. His head shook back and forth as if he couldn't believe what he had heard. He took the certificate in both hands, looked down at it, and then placed it on the counter as he tapped it with his fingers. Then he pushed it closer to my mother. He continued to glare at her as he said, "Fine, your choice." He turned his back on my mother. "Abby, where would you like to go?"

"Turner's maybe," I squeaked out. At that moment, all I wanted was to get out of the kitchen.

"Let's go," my father said. I walked toward the back door with my father close behind me. I stepped onto the driveway and looked back at him. He stood there for the longest minute, looking back into the kitchen, and then pulled the door closed.

A thousand pins of light were pricking my body from head to toe. What just happened? The cool night air calmed me down a little. I stood by the car door while my father slapped his hands against every pocket he had and then did it again looking for his keys. Finally, he yanked them out of his jacket pocket and hit the unlock button. Once I heard the rumble inside the door, I opened it and slid onto the front seat.

Usually, my father chattered nonstop when we were alone. Tonight he was quiet. At a stoplight he turned toward me. "Sorry about that, honey. I don't like to have you hear me argue with your mother."

"It's okay, Dad." My shoulders loosened a little.

"No, it's not. I'm sorry your mother didn't come with us." That wasn't exactly how I felt. I was glad she didn't come and glad he stuck up for me. The line of traffic in front of us started up. "Sometimes parents disagree about how to handle their kids. Usually, your mother and I talk about those things in private and come to an agreement. I don't know what happened tonight."

Flashes of light from the streetlamps slid over the front window of the car like a golden dotted line. My father and I didn't talk for the rest of the trip to the restaurant. When we strolled to the front door, he asked, "Hungry?"

"Yeah, a little," I said.

"After all that work on your project, you should be starved," he said as he pulled open the glass door of the restaurant.

"Yeah, you're right about that." Somehow the good feeling I had when I first told him about winning had disappeared. Instead something yucky was sloshing around in the bottom of my empty stomach. Not a fun feeling.

After we got settled at our table and the waitress had given us menus, I looked at my dad. His face reminded me of a word we had talked about in language arts—*plaintive*. It meant sad or melancholy. Yeah, my dad definitely looked plaintive. I wanted to ask him about what he said to my mother about *her* mother. Something told me this wasn't the time, so I decided to talk about school to take his mind off what happened at home.

"So, Dad, I was thinking of joining the chess club at school. Or the photography club. I'm not sure yet which one."

His eyes lit up. "No kidding. If you join the chess club, we could play together."

"You play chess?" I said. "I didn't know that."

"Yep, started in high school and stayed with it in college. I found it very relaxing." He got that look he had when he talked about being in high school or college. Like he was recalling a good memory.

"That's cool. That we could play together, I mean." There was so much about my dad that I didn't know.

"And if you join the photography club, you can use my camera." That would be the camera he got for

Father's Day that sits on a shelf in the front closet. For sure, he used it one time to take a picture of Shelly and me and then put it away. He must have lost interest or something.

"Cool, Dad. Thanks."

"You know, honey, that's a smart thing to do—joining a club that could lead to a hobby. Both of those would be things you could do well into adulthood."

"Well, I was thinking of things that I could do as a kid, Dad."

"That too, honey. Don't want to grow up too fast, right?" He managed a half smile.

I smiled back, and the waitress arrived to take our order. After she left, my father said, "You're only having a salad? Aren't you hungry?"

"Not really."

"This hasn't turned out to be such a great celebration. I'm sorry, kiddo." He fiddled with his knife.

"No, it's great, Dad, really." I could tell he wasn't convinced.

While we waited for our food, I looked up and saw a woman who looked a lot like my mother standing at the front of the restaurant, looking around the room.

It was my mother! "Dad, Mom's here!"

He turned around to look over his shoulder and then stood up and walked toward her. They stood close to each other right near the place where the lady who showed you to your seat stood. At first, he looked upset, almost angry. What if they continued to argue right here where everyone in the restaurant would hear them? I held my breath. My dad put his hand on my mother's upper arm and squeezed it gently and then slipped it around her waist as he guided her toward our table. I let out my breath.

As she got close to the table, I noticed that her face looked a little softer than when we were in the kitchen. I wasn't sure what to do, so I waited for her to say something. "Hi. Is it okay if I join you?"

I nodded. She slid across the seat opposite me, and my father moved in beside her.

My mother put her eyes right on me. "Abby, what happened at home …" She placed her fingers over her mouth and tapped her lips several times. "I don't know if I can explain this, but I'd like to try."

I looked at my father, and he nodded, so I did too.

"When I was growing up, my mother's way of dealing with me was different from how my friends' parents did it. I can remember seeing my friends' parents get all excited when they showed them their papers from school, even simple things like a weekly spelling test when they got a really good grade. Their mothers would hug them and say how proud they were, and their fathers would smile and give them a high five or pat them on the back. I never had that from either my mother or father. I'm not even sure my mother looked at my papers from school. She never even asked about school or how I was doing. Until I met your father, I never really knew what it was like to have someone be interested in me." My father squeezed her shoulder with one hand and put the other over her hands.

"I remember one time when I was in fourth or fifth grade, I won a contest in school like you did. A spelling contest, I think. I ran into the house with my ribbon to show to my mother. When I gave it to her, she asked, 'What's this?' I told her about winning the contest, that I was first out of all the kids in my grade, both classes. She handed it back to me and said, 'Strange way of teaching, if you ask me. Giving out prizes to children who do what they are supposed to do anyway. Go get changed. I need you to set the table for supper.' She turned away from me and never gave me a compliment after that. When she died fifteen years ago, I never knew what she thought about anything I did. I never even knew if she loved me."

My mother's eyes watered. She bent her head.

This whole thing was beginning to seem like a dream. "Sorry, Mom." I didn't know what to do, what to say. I had never seen my mother cry, had never heard her say anything like this before. My father moved his hand back and forth across her shoulder as she fumbled for a tissue. "Thanks for coming." That sounded real lame, but it was the only thing that I could come up with.

My mother smiled as she dotted her eyes with the tissue she pulled from her pocketbook. "So," she continued, lifting the glass of water the waitress had put in front of her, "here's to you and Eden for the great job you did on your project." My father raised his glass and clinked it against hers.

"Thanks," I said. Something inside me broke open as if someone had pried the lock on a treasure box, and when the top burst open, this whole new feeling jumped out. I was glad that my mother was there. That was new, different. I wasn't totally sure what to think about it, about her.

When the waitress brought our food, I decided to order a burger with fries. Suddenly, I was starved.

Chapter 11

What would the pack do now that we had won? Instead of congratulating myself for winning, all I thought about the next morning as I got ready for school was what they would do to get back at me and Eden because we outdid them. It will probably be worse now, much worse! As I pulled on my socks and shoes, though, a different feeling sat next to my fear—something less panicky, maybe calmer.

Another thing I thought about was my mother's confession about her mother never giving her any praise when she was a kid. That was so huge, but it didn't prepare me to see her in the kitchen at seven o'clock in the morning.

"Mom, what are you doing up so early?"

"I decided to check on you considering all that happened between us yesterday. You okay with everything?"

I wasn't sure how to answer, but I said, "Yeah, I'm good."

"Would you like some juice?" She put down her coffee mug and waited for me to answer.

"Sure, that would be great." While she moved around the kitchen, I put cereal in a bowl and poured milk over it. I decided not to make any comments since she had tried so hard yesterday to be honest with me. Besides, I was not really sure what to say—something funny, something sarcastic. I kept my mouth shut and chewed.

"By the way, I have to shop for some things at the mall on the way home from work tonight. Would you like me to pick up a few tops for you to wear to school? I think I have a good idea of your size."

"Sure. Thanks, Mom"

"I'll probably pick some brighter colors for you to liven up your coloring."

I wondered if she wanted me to come along. "Should I come along with you?"

"Not this time. It would mean coming all the way out here first and then going back toward the mall. It's faster if I do it on the way home from work. Dad will be home in time to get supper started."

"Okay. I'd better help him with supper. You know how he is when he gets near a stove."

My mother looked over at me and smiled. "Indeed I do." She pulled open the cabinet door where the phone numbers were listed. "Fire department's number listed here just in case," she said as she pointed to the sheet of paper. "Top number."

I gave her a thumbs-up and then grabbed my backpack. "Gotta go. See ya."

"Have a good day," she said over her coffee mug.

That was the first time I ever heard her say that to me. Then this warm feeling rushed into my chest.

✵ ✵ ✵

"Hey, Abby, cool project," someone said over my shoulder as I stood at my locker in school. On the bus and in the hallways, kids coming at me in all directions yelled about how much they liked our project. My locker was plastered with sheets of paper with congratulations printed large in all kinds of fancy, colorful letters. This whole thing was beginning to feel like a dream. I couldn't wait to see how Eden's day was going.

Then my mind did a tricky thing. In a split second, my really good feeling was washed away by this scary darkness. Okay, where were *they?* When would *they* attack? There it was. My fear was back! One thing I was pretty sure about was that they would be sneakier than before. They wouldn't want anyone to see them being mean to me. "Hey, Abby, you should sit at our table for lunch." Two girls said behind me as I stood at my locker and pulled out books for class. I nodded but knew I would search out Eden. In a sense, this was like having a little more protection than before. There were more kids on my side. That felt good and bad at the same time—good because I had it and bad because it probably made the pack angrier.

Since he spent those days in the hospital, Eden never had time to come up with a new plan to help me avoid the pack, so I decided to avoid them if I could. It seemed to work pretty well up to lunchtime. When I rushed to my locker, trying to beat them down the hallway to the lunchroom, my hands got all clumsy, so the books inside my locker somehow slid onto the floor. When I finally got everything packed neatly into my locker and shut the door, I stood in the corridor, alone.

My insides knotted up. I hated being such a wimp. As I walked toward the stairway, I tensed up every time I came to an open classroom door. I expected *them* to jump out at me. I took a deep breath and shot past each door as fast as possible. Halfway down the corridor, I heard some giggling, but when I turned around to look, no one was there. It must have been my imagination playing tricks on me. Finally, I reached the stairs to the first floor. No problem so far. I turned the doorknob and found the door moving without my help, being pulled from the other side. There they were—Stephanie, Karen, and Jen! Funny thing, though, was that Michelle wasn't there.

Not only were they mean, but they were big. They formed a semicircle around me so I had to put my back against the wall. *Here goes—same people, different stairwell.* What were they going to do this time?

"So, look who's here, guys," Stephanie said. "Our first-prize winner. Bet you think you're pretty smart now, don't you?" she said at my face.

My legs wobbled a little, but I kept quiet and didn't look at her.

"But you know what?" she continued. "We think if it wasn't for your sidekick, you'd never have won. Right, guys?" She looked at her pack members.

"Yeah, you're not smart enough to win anything, pea brain," Karen said as she hit the back of my head. My glasses almost fell off.

"So anyway," Stephanie said. "We have a message for you. What do you think about the principal getting a note that tells him you did hardly any work on the project, that it was all your partner's work. Course, it won't be signed, but I think it might cause a commotion. What do you think, guys?"

"I wouldn't want to answer a charge like that. It could be hard to explain your way through it," said Karen.

Eden would never go for this. If I told him, he'd want to come after them. I couldn't let that happen. "But that's not true," I managed to squeak out.

"Doesn't matter if it's true or not," Stephanie said as she pushed her face close to mine. "It's what's going to happen. Get it?"

"Eden won't say something is true if it's not!" Words spilled out of my mouth before I had a chance to think about what I was saying.

"Let's just say I wouldn't want to be you." Stephanie had a way of lowering her voice to make what she said sound more threatening. "Come on, guys. I'm starved," she said. Karen and Jen followed her down the stairs like little puppies. Their laughter bounced off the walls as they went down. Once the door to the corridor below slammed shut behind them, my insides shook for a minute before I was able to relax. I let my back slide down the wall until I was sitting on the floor.

Strange how the quiet in the stairwell seemed like it was shouting at me, telling me I was totally alone. All the good feelings from that morning were gone. Here I was, a first-prize winner, all bunched up on the floor of the stairwell like a pile of dirt that people would step over. I got up and went back through the door into the hallway to check the clock. There was still time left for the lunch period, so I decided to stay where I was until I heard the other kids returning to class. I sat on the floor under the clock, hugging my knees. Suddenly, I was tired; I was really tired of being pushed around.

✳ ✳ ✳

His eyes darted back and forth like a Ping-Pong ball in motion. "You're kidding. You know what? I'm really tired of those losers." I was not surprised he couldn't believe what I told him about Stephanie's challenge. We sat at his kitchen table, facing each other. "They're gonna tell Mr. Winters that you didn't contribute to the project?"

"That's what they said."

Uh-oh, he was getting mad. I was afraid that would happen. "They think they can run around the school, threatening anyone and get away with it." His knees knocked against each other as he swung them back and forth. "Okay, they want to challenge me. Well, let's see how it works out." His voice was getting louder. He did not look at me as he talked. "I know what I'm gonna do. I'm gonna threaten *them*. I'll tell them if they don't leave you alone that *I'm* gonna go to the principal. Then we'll see what they do about that."

"Eeds, no, this is not your problem," I said. If he let this bother him, it could mean he'd end up back in the hospital. "It's time for me to do something. I have to stand up to them!" I didn't feel as brave as I sounded.

"Okay, do you have a plan?" At least he wasn't as excited as before.

"No, I don't have a plan. But you know what? You're right. If I don't do something, this is gonna go on for the next three years." What I did not say to him was that I had no idea how to make them stop. I didn't even know what to say or how to act. One thing was for sure. I was getting a lot of practice at being scared.

"Hey, maybe I can help you." He moved the lever on his chair so it moved to a position where he could face me.

"How?" I perked up.

"I don't want you to take this the wrong way, Abs," he said as he raised his hands toward me like people did when they wanted to tell you something they thought you did not want to hear. "But we have to work on your toughness. It's not that you *aren't* tough. You just don't *sound* tough. Why do you think Stephanie can lead the other three around so easy?" He waited for me to think that over.

"She talks tough so the others think she really is. But you know what? I'll bet if you got her alone, you'd find out she's really a wimp without them. So, we have to figure out a way for you to get her alone."

"Are you serious? Me alone with the queen of the pack? Even if I do get her by herself, I don't know how to get her to stop bothering me."

His eyes lit up. "Okay, let's practice." He moved his wheelchair closer so our knees were almost touching. "All right, I'm Stephanie," he said. "And you and I are alone. Okay, go"

Nothing came out of my mouth. It was like my tongue was paralyzed or something.

"Go ahead, Abs. Say something."

"I can't do it this way. It feels weird."

"Okay, I'll start." He closed his eyes for a minute like he was meditating. Then his eyes flipped open. "Well, if it isn't stupid Abby." He leaned forward. "Hey, what do you want?" He had this attitude. He was really getting into this.

Once again, my tongue sat like a lump of clay in my mouth. He looked at me, waiting. "Okay, Abs, tell me what you're feeling right now."

"Frustrated. I can't get my tongue to move because my brain's not telling my mouth what to say."

"Okay, I get that, but how do you feel? When you

meet Stephanie, what's the feeling that comes over you, like right away, even before she says anything?"

"Scared. Whenever I meet her or them, I feel scared."

"See, now that's what we've got to work on. Don't you ever feel angry when you meet up with them?"

"Yeah." I did not want to admit this because it showed what a big coward I was, that I was afraid to defend myself when someone made me angry.

"When?" He kept pushing. Couldn't he see that I didn't want to do this?

"I don't know. When they hit me or kick me, I guess." I picked at my fingers.

"So, what do you do when they make you angry?"

"Nothing."

"Nothing! What do you mean, Abs? When they hit you, you don't want to hit back or something?"

"I want to, but I'm afraid to." Now he knew that I was a big wuss.

"Oh, okay, so you think if you do, they'll jump all over you, right?"

"Yeah, pretty much." Talking about this wasn't getting us anywhere.

"How about if it was just you and Stephanie. Would you be afraid then?"

"Not as much, I guess. But I don't know how to

stand up to her." I sat back in my chair. "I mean, what do I say when we're standing there face-to-face? 'Hey, Stephanie, keep your hands off me.' Like she's just gonna turn around and walk away from me after I say that, probably laughing the whole time."

"Okay, so what if she does? What could you say back to her that would make a difference? Come on. Let's practice it."

"Eeds, I don't want to talk about this anymore." That was so not like me. I usually always cooperated.

"Don't stop now, Abs. Let's keep going. We're getting close."

I let out a sigh. "Okay, what's next?"

"All right, you're alone with Stephanie and she says, 'What's with you, turd?' and you say something like, 'You keep away from me.' But she says, 'Or what?' Now what do you say back to her?"

"I say, 'So long, Stephanie.' Come on, Eeds. Don't you get it. I don't know what to say after that." As I said each word, I punched my thigh.

"Okay, I'm Stephanie again. 'So, what do you think you can do to me? I could sneeze on you, and you'd fall over.' Now, Abs, say something that tells her you're not gonna let her do it again, that you're gonna fight back. Just say the words. Don't worry right now if you can do it or not."

"Then we can stop?"

"Yep, just do this last thing."

I pushed myself up to look like I was challenging Stephanie. "I don't know what I'm gonna do, but I'm sure not gonna let you push me around anymore."

"Right words. Now say it like you mean it, Abs. Sound more angry!"

"I am sounding angry. Why do you keep saying that?" He was really starting to bug me.

Now he was Stephanie again. "You're not gonna let me push you around. Ha! You're such a baby. You wouldn't even stand up to an ant. Baby, baby ..." All of a sudden, he slapped my knees and then pushed my shoulders. What the heck was he doing? "Come on, little baby Abby. Can't defend yourself?" he said as he jabbed my shoulders. It was a light punch, but still. At first, I didn't know what to do. However, he kept doing it, poking my arms, my legs, my shoulders. I didn't know how to get him to stop. I raised my hands so he couldn't get at my shoulders, but his slapping and hitting kept coming. *What's wrong with him?* I thought. *Has he flipped?*

"Eeds," I shouted, "stop it! What are you doing? Why are you hitting me?" I crossed my arms in front of my face, but he kept doing it. "Are you crazy? What's wrong with you? Stop it!"

He hit faster and faster. I didn't even have a chance to think. I started to get scared! Maybe he was having some kind of a fit connected to his sickness. "Eeds, stop it. Leave me alone." I tried to get up, but he pressed one hand down on my shoulders and used the other to poke me. His slapping was light, but he wouldn't stop.

"Come on, baby Abby. Can't stick up for yourself? Can't stop me, can you? I thought so. You are a baby." Then he started to chant, "Abby's a baby. Abby's a baby."

I was not a baby. Why was he saying that? I thought he understood. I thought he was my friend. He'd better stop hitting me. He'd better get away from me! I'd had enough of this crap! Just because he was in a chair didn't mean he could do this to me. I managed to slide my hands through his, grab his shoulders, and shove him against the back of his chair. Then I stood up, got hold of his arms, and held them up in the air, squeezing his wrists, hoping that would stop him. "Leave me alone," I shouted. "Leave me alone! Stop it!" I looked down into his eyes, waiting for him to stop pushing against my hands.

"Okay, Abs. Okay, I got it." He shook his hands to show he was giving in, smiled up at me, and then laughed. "I knew it was in there. Your anger came out, Abs. Cool!"

What was he saying about anger? I straightened up and let his hands go. But I stood there for a minute, waiting for the next slap. "What? What are you talking about? Why were you hitting me?"

"To get you to make your anger come out. It worked! You got mad at me. How did it feel?"

"I didn't like it. I don't like getting angry at you."

"No, but you did because I kept it up. That made you angry, so you defended yourself. Ha!" He formed two fists and stuck his thumbs in the air.

"You did it on purpose … to make me angry?" What was that all about?

"Yep!" His smile was so wide that you could hardly see the rest of his face.

"What good does my getting angry do?" I sat down.

"So, you'll know how to feel the next time Stephanie pushes or kicks you."

"Oh," I said, still confused.

Then he said, "So want some snacks?"

That didn't fit with what we were talking about. I blinked. My mind was still back on why he did this. He didn't get that I couldn't try to fight her. I didn't have enough strength to overpower her. So, she could still pulverize me and leave me in the dust. There I would be, this tiny pile of anger lying on the floor all smeared in blood. I reached into the plastic bag of pretzels he held out and stuffed some into my mouth. At least if we were eating, we wouldn't have to talk about this anymore.

✳ ✳ ✳

That night I sat on my bed, thinking about what Eeds and I had practiced. It got me thinking about what people, especially Stephanie, see when they look at me. I closed my eyes and imagined myself being Stephanie when she first saw me in the hallway at school. There I was, a short kid with frizzy hair and glasses who acts *scared* of everything. To her, I was a perfect target. It's like there's a sign on me that says, "Pick on me. I don't fight back."

There was one question I had to find an answer to. Since I wasn't big enough to overpower Stephanie, what could I threaten her with that would keep her away from me? Even though she couldn't stand Mr. Gibson, she always acted nice to him, and he lapped it up. The only way I could change that would be to tell him a lie about her. If I do that, though, then I'd be just like her.

Okay, since she walked around the school acting like the queen of middle school, pretending to be like a kid with super school spirit and smiling at the principal, I'd bet she wouldn't like it if I told him about all the things she and her pack have done to me. She'd go ballistic if I did that. She might come after me even after I told him. But if she knew I'd go back to him every time she did something to me, that would probably keep her away. But do I have the courage to do that? *Face it*, I thought. *I'm afraid of my own shadow. Will I ever change? Will I always let people push me around like she does?* Sadness crawled into my stomach and sat down, kind of like a cat plopping itself down in a favorite spot, waiting until someone who didn't want it there any more pushed it away.

When my eyelids flipped open, my eyes fixed on the Spider Woman poster on my wall that Shelly had given me. She looked like I wanted to feel—strong and fierce. Maybe I could convince myself to feel that way. All I have to do was tell myself I was strong. I could make up a chant to say whenever I saw the pack, something like "I am strong, and I can stand up to them." If I kept saying it over and over, pretty soon I'd be convinced that it was true. As I hugged my stuffed rhinoceros, I noticed how the muscles in my arm kind of stood up when I made a fist. Strange how I never even noticed that before.

Chapter 12

It was getting cold out. October was almost over, and Halloween was a few days away. You could feel the excitement around school. Kids talked nonstop about what they were going to do that night.

Last year Shelly and I went trick-or-treating together dressed as salt and pepper shakers. I remember how hard it was to walk inside a tube of cardboard. Shelly was pepper, and I was salt. We put white dots all over our bicycle helmets for the cap of the shaker. When people opened their doors and saw us, they would burst out laughing as they dropped piles of candy into our bags.

I could not imagine Eden trick-or-treating, so I never brought it up. Since I had no other friends, I expected to spend the night at home. The day before Halloween, I was thinking about this as I got off the bus and trudged up the driveway to the back door. As soon as I got inside, the phone rang. "Hey, Abs," Eden said, "since I don't go out trick-or-treating, I was thinking about doing something here for the kids who come to our house. Want to help me?"

"Sure! What're you gonna do?"

"Dress up and scare them or make them laugh when the door opens."

I liked both ideas. "Cool! Do you have something to make a costume with?"

"Right now, my mom is looking through a bag of old clothes and curtains for material. Come on over."

We probably wouldn't have time to work on homework. I left my books on the table and ran outside and up the ramp to his back door.

In the kitchen, Eden held up a pair of heavy curtains, a silver- and gray-colored material with a shine to it. "Look at this! My mom said we could cut these up if we want to."

"Eeds, I just thought of something. If we can find a big box, we could make you into a robot. The little kids will love it."

"How?"

"We make holes in the box for your arms and legs, but it will sit on your chair. Then we cover the box with the material and use construction paper for buttons and lights. We could even attach some giant-size nuts and bolts from my father's workbench for knobs."

"Hey, great! What about you? What will you wear," Eden asked.

"I don't know. Let's do yours first."

His mother found a box in the basement that was the perfect size. We turned it sideways and cut the bottom out so it would rest on the seat of his chair. Then we cut a piece out of the back so he could sit against his chair without having the box move. We cut two semicircle holes on the bottom edge for his legs and two full holes in the sides for his arms. In the front we put a slit for his eyes. Finally, I stapled the material to the box, sliced out the eyehole, and taped the material inside. Using a black magic marker, I drew lines for sections of the robot's body and made dots for those steel things that are like nails used to keep pieces of steel together. Eden had gray pants and a gray shirt to cover his arms and legs, and he would wear gray or black gloves on his hands. Then I had this great idea. If we had a set of Christmas tree lights, the ones that go on and off automatically, we could tape them to the box and plug them in whenever kids came to the door for a really cool effect. I was pretty sure my dad would let us use some of ours.

"Hey, Abs, this is perfect. Did you think of anything for yourself yet?"

"No, but I will by tomorrow."

That night while my dad searched in the attic for the lights for Eden's costume, I decided my costume would be a space alien. That way we would look sort of like a unit.

"Abby, what are you going to do for a costume for tonight?" my mother asked.

"I'm going to be a space alien to go with Eden's robot. Can I use your black winter gloves to go with my black outfit?"

"Yes, I'll get them. What else do you need?"

"I'm gonna make a mask, but I need something for my head, you know, to cover my hair."

"Hmm. How about that hat you got for Christmas last year that you didn't like. It's dark, and you can tuck your hair under it pretty easily." It was nice having her help—nice and new.

"Yeah, cool. Could I glue some glitter on it?"

"I don't see why not. You might as well get some wear out of it," she said.

For a mask I cut an oval out of cardboard with very large, pointy ears on the side and long, sharp eyeholes on the front. With a magic marker, I made a pointy nose and a mouth like a zipper. For the top, I cut a V-shaped piece out of cardboard to be an antenna. I also spread glitter across a large piece of cardboard that I would wear on my chest to match the head covering. To finish my costume off, I made a wand with an aluminum foil star on the top and shiny ribbon streamers. Even though I had to stay up late to finish my homework, it went pretty fast because I was in a much better mood.

✼ ✼ ✼

On Halloween night we stationed ourselves at Eden's front door. Whenever the bell rang, I opened the door, and Eden moved his chair forward so he could be seen. Most times the kids would forget to say, "Trick or treat," for a minute as they stared at the blinking lights. Then they would make some comment or just stick their trick-or-treat bags out for the loot.

"Hey, dude, cool costume," one older kid said. "Is the chair part of it?"

"Nah, it goes where I go. Hey, yours is pretty good too," Eden said. "Here, have a treat."

Whenever a little kid showed up, it became an opportunity for Eden to mess around. One kid who was about three feet high said from inside his spaceman outfit, "Hey, a robot!"

Eden shot back, "Yep, that's what I am, a robot." The lights sparkled on and off, on and off all over the top and sides of his costume. The kid stood there, staring.

"Robots can't talk," the little kid said. He sounded pretty sure about that.

"Who told you that?" Eden asked. "Robots can do lots of things that people can do, sometimes even better. Just because you never heard a robot talk like me doesn't mean they can't."

I watched the eyeholes in the little kid's mask. His eyes blinked several times like he was thinking about what Eden said. Then he turned around and waddled down the walk. He wasn't hanging around. His nearly empty trick-or-treat bag went plop, plop, plop as it banged against his legs.

"Hey, don't you want any treats?" Eden yelled.

"Not from a liar."

Eden backed his chair away from the open door, and when I closed it, he laughed so hard his costume shook up and down. "Hey, Abs, that was a blast!"

After two more trick-or-treaters, we ran out of candy, so we shut the porch light off. "Hey, nobody from our grade came tonight," Eden said.

"Nope."

"Maybe they didn't come up this far. We could go down the street a little way and check it out. Want to?"

I was only kind of interested, but I could tell he really wanted to do it. "I don't know, Eeds. What will your parents say?"

"C'mon, I'll ask."

After I removed the string of lights from his costume, I followed him into the living room.

"Hey, guys, Abs and I want to go down the street a little way to see if there are any kids from school on our street. You okay with that?"

"I don't know, Eeds," his mother said. "It's dark out there. You have to stay on this side of the street, no crossing over."

"Remember," his father added, "drivers can't see you that well in your wheelchair, and kids are up to all kinds of mischief tonight. I'm not sure it's such a good idea. You know what? I think I should go with you." He stood up and folded his newspaper.

"*Dad*, if you come with me and we meet kids we know, it'll look like I can't go out without a babysitter. Come on, just this one night," the robot said, begging.

"I can't believe I'm trying to reason with a box," his father said. He stuck his hands deep inside his pockets.

"Be back in half an hour, or I'll come looking for you," his father warned.

"C'mon, Dad, by the time we get to the corner,

we'll have to turn right around. Give us a little more time. We'll stop at the house after Abs's house. We won't go all the way to the corner. Two houses away."

"Here," his father said, pulling his cell phone out of his pocket. He looked at the cell phone screen. "It's 8:30 now. Be back here by 9:15 at the latest. If you aren't, I come looking for you. Got it?"

"Got it! Thanks." Eden took the phone, lifted his costume, and stuffed it into his pocket. Then he moved the lever on his chair and turned it toward the kitchen.

Suddenly, I felt nervous about this whole thing. Deep down I wished they had not said yes.

I shivered as we stepped into the cool air on the back deck. Eden's costume stayed in place as the chair wheels moved down the ramp. I congratulated myself that we had designed it right. At the end of the driveway, we turned left toward the corner.

Darkness surrounded us like a dense, thick fog. If it weren't for the whir of Eden's chair motor, I would have sworn he had disappeared. Somewhere in the blackness, a dog howled like they did when something was wrong. The house on the other side of mine was unlit, so we had to move through a long, dark stretch. Voices came from pretty far down the street, but I couldn't see anyone. The bushes next to my shoulder moved like there was some thing or someone on the other side walking along with us. Whatever it was, I wasn't going to let it attack me. I ran around to the other side of Eden's chair just in case. Then I felt guilty. I was supposed to be protecting him! I moved over behind his chair but kept to the middle of the sidewalk. Man, if someone jumped us, I wouldn't be much help. Suddenly, the leaves above my head flapped wildly. Was something moving through them? A shiver crawled up my back. I felt cold, uncomfortable. "Hey, Eeds, let's go back. There's no one out here. Everyone's gone home."

"You're kidding, Abs. This is great! I never get a chance to be out without my parents at night." His chair moved faster. There was no way he was turning back.

From the corner, moonlight fell on four tall, dark figures walking toward us. I tuned into their voices but couldn't hear much. As they got closer, one of them said, "Let's not go up there. I don't want to get in trouble." It was Michelle's voice!

My heart skipped a beat. *The pack!* Oh, man, we had to turn back!

"Oh, my god, Michelle, you're such a baby. What makes you think we're gonna get into trouble?" I was right. That was Stephanie!

"What are you gonna do when you find their house?" Michelle asked.

"I don't know. I'll decide when I come to it. Wait. I

just thought of something." She bent down near a bush and picked up a small rock. "Hey, guys, find a rock. What do you think about saying happy Halloween with a broken window?"

"Sounds great," Karen said.

"What a nice surprise," Jen said.

"Wait. We're gonna break windows?" cried Michelle. "I'm not doing that. I don't want to get in trouble."

"Fine, Michelle. Don't throw a rock then. Now come on."

At this point, there was only a driveway between us. The streetlamp across the street reflected off Eden's wheelchair. Suddenly, the four of them stopped, and so did we. "What luck, guys," Stephanie said to the other three. "Here are the two people we came to wish a happy Halloween to, dumb Abby and the roller turd. So isn't this too cute—a robot and a space alien."

"Hey," Eden said, "I'm glad you dropped by, Stephanie. I got your message about telling the principal that Abby didn't do anything on the project. Well, guess what? It's not true. So, you can forget about leaving a note for the principal."

Suddenly, my legs felt weak like they were going to give way. This was not starting out so well. Eden might get hurt. I needed to stop him from walking straight into it. I bent over his shoulder and said in a low voice, "Eeds, come on. Let's go back."

"No, Abs, we're gonna have this out right here." He raised the box over his head and dropped it onto the sidewalk. "So, come on, big shot Stephanie. What are you gonna do to me? What? You've got a rock in your hand? Gonna knock me out?"

What was he doing? Oh, my god, this was not good! "Eeds, I mean it. Let's go." This time I said it louder, but he and Stephanie were locked in a battle of their own. He never even heard me.

"I don't pick on kids in wheelchairs. Just their friends," Stephanie replied. "So, since you decided not to back up our story, that must mean you'd rather have us come after her. Some friend you are." She dragged out the last thing she said in a sarcastic tone.

"Don't change the topic," Eden shot back. "You won't pick on me because you're afraid to." For a split second, no one said anything. Why was he challenging her? There were four of them and two of us, and he was in a wheelchair!

Stephanie stepped forward and put her hands on her hips. "I'm afraid of *you*? Ha! You can't even stand up. Why should I be afraid of you?"

"Good question." Eden's voice was very calm. He pushed his shoulders forward. "Why are you?"

I couldn't believe it! Every time he opened his mouth, things got worse. "Let's go back, Eeds," I said, begging him.

Stephanie turned to her pack. "This guy can't be for real. He thinks he could beat me in a fight."

"Must be crazy," Jen said.

"Doesn't value his life maybe," Karen chimed in.

It felt like a stage was being set for a fight scene and I couldn't stop it. Even if I did go back for Eden's father, by the time we came back, he'd probably be really hurt. I had to stay and try to help him.

"Yeah, he's as crazy as dumb Abby," Stephanie said. She leaned over, put her hands on the arms of Eden's chair, and pushed her face close to his. "So, roller freak, what can you do to me that's gonna hurt?"

With that, Eden grabbed Stephanie's wrists. She made this hissing sound. With the light on her face, I could see her gritting her teeth. Suddenly, she dropped the rock in her hand, spread her arms out, pulled back, and lifted her foot. In a lightning-fast move, she jammed her heel into Eden's crotch. Suddenly, he let her wrists go and bent over, covering the area where her foot had hit him. That gave her enough time to charge around behind his chair. In seconds, she had yanked his body back and circled her arm around his neck in a headlock. He started to rise slightly out of his chair. It shook a little then with all that weight on the back. Suddenly, it lost balance and fell to the side. Eden's body spilled onto the ground. Stephanie wasted no time. She crouched over him and pulled him away from the chair and against her stomach. He looked kind of lifeless. I could not tell if he was conscious or not. Stephanie was down on her knees with her arm around his neck. She continued to squeeze.

I stood there, my feet like two heavy lead blocks, frozen in fear. Suddenly, Eden came to life. He grabbed Stephanie's arm and tried to peel it off his neck. His other arm just sat by his side, not moving. She attached her other hand to her wrist to tighten her grip. She grunted as she pulled him farther away from his chair. Then he started to breathe heavy like he couldn't get enough air. His legs stretched out from his body with no movement in them. Oh, my god, he was going to die! In my mind, I saw his father's face looking at me. I had to get her off him!

A switch clicked on inside me, and this other person jumped out of my skin and burst to life. My wand fell to the ground as I yanked off my mask and bent over Stephanie. With my two hands around her left arm, I used all my strength to pull her away from Eden. It didn't work! Stephanie's body was rigid. It had become permanently attached to Eden. I made a fist and pushed out the knuckles of my middle finger so it was hard and pointy like a weapon. I kept punching the arm Stephanie had around Eden's neck hard several times until it finally broke free. Then I grabbed her jacket collar, held onto her arm, and dragged her totally free of Eden. She reached behind her neck and tried to force my hands free, but I moved so fast she couldn't make it happen. Her body moved all over the ground as she tried to get control of me, but I kept myself clear of her.

A new spirit had come to life inside me. I was this new strong person! I also knew that she was taller than I was, so I had to work fast to get on top of her and pin her down. I put my hands against her shoulders and slammed her to the ground. While she recovered from the surprise, I planted a knee on the ground on each side of her body. Using the lower part of her arms, she started this wild punching thing at my sides, yelling, "Get off me! Get off me!" When she tried to reach my stomach, I bent down and drew my elbows in to protect myself. Then almost without thinking, I grabbed both her wrists and slammed them against the sidewalk on each side of her head. My face was directly above hers. Now I was in control.

I heard scuffling behind me. "Steph, what do you want us to do?" one of the pack members shouted. I thought they'd be all over me, but it turned out they never did anything unless Stephanie gave an order.

She lifted her head slightly and shouted back, "Shut up!"

She struggled to get out from beneath me, but I sat on her stomach. With my hands holding her wrists down, I held her so tight she couldn't move the top part of her body. "If you do something like that to Eden or *me* ever again, I will be all over you. No matter where— in the hallways at school, on the bus, or on the street. I'm *sick* of you shoving me, kicking me, and making fun of me. No more! No more! You understand? I'm *done* with it! You stay away from me. Leave me alone." These words poured out of my mouth like someone else was saying them. Nothing came from Stephanie. "I said do you understand me?" I shouted that right in her face.

Her head moved slightly. I took that for a yes.

"Now I'm gonna get off you. If you make one move to do anything, I promise you we'll end up on the ground again." I was about to let her arms go, and then I thought of something else. "One more thing, on Monday, *I'm* going to the principal's office, and I'm gonna tell him what you've been doing to me for the last two months. If you come after me after that, I'll go back to him every time. Even if your pack lies for you, he'll know about you. You hear me?"

"Yes," she stammered. "Now get off me!" She pushed her weight against my hands.

I waited a few seconds and then pulled myself off her and stood up quickly. She sat up, rubbed her wrists, and then pushed herself to a standing position. After brushing her arms and legs, she turned directly toward me. "You're a little creep!" She sneered. That was for her pack. She needed to have them think she was still in charge.

I raised myself to my full height with my face as close to hers as I could get it. My fists were so tight I could feel my nails digging into the skin. "And you're nothing but a big *wimp*," I said the last word extra loud and extra deep. She was about to say something but did not. "Get out of here," I shouted, "and take them with you." I backed away from Stephanie but kept my arms stiff with my fists clenched. If she wanted to start something else, I was ready.

"Come on," Stephanie said to the others. "Why waste our time on these two losers."

I watched them walk silently into the darkness. Strange how they looked at me but didn't make any rude comments or at least laugh like they usually do. I took a deep breath.

Eden rested on one elbow and looked up at me. "Man, you were awesome!"

"Yeah? I didn't feel awesome. Mostly scared at first when she got you in a headlock. Then, like, so angry."

"If my chair didn't fall over, I could have taken her," he said. "What she doesn't realize is that my upper body strength is pretty fierce because I exercise it so much. But when you got her down, I knew it was your fight." I knew that was only partly true. When she squeezed his throat, he couldn't catch his breath. But I decided not to say anything.

"So, are you okay? What's wrong with your arm?"

"It's okay," he said, shaking it. "Just a little numb from falling on it."

"We'd better call your father." I bent down to help him up.

"Why?" He was sitting up on the sidewalk, rubbing his arm.

"To help you get in your chair," I said.

"Naw, I can do it myself. C'mon, I'll show you. Bring my chair over here."

I turned the chair up on its wheels.

"Okay, now turn the seat to face me and lock the front wheels with that lever," he said, pointing to a metal piece on the side of the small front wheels. He turned his hands onto the sidewalk, turned his body, and pushed against them until his rear end was partway up. He was right about being strong. The muscles in his skinny arms bulged when he pushed against them, and his knees inched forward. He reached up and curved his hands around the side of the seat and then pressed hard against his elbows to raise his body up. He was kneeling now. Then he moved his hands up to the arms of the chair and continued to push. He slowly raised his body up until he was standing.

"You okay, Eeds?" I asked. "What do you need me to do?"

He took a deep breath. From what little light there was, I could see sweat spread across his forehead. "Hold the back of the chair. I'll do the rest."

I put my hands around the rubber handles on the back of the chair and waited. I never took my eyes off him. He stood facing me with all his weight on the arms of the chair. I couldn't see how he was going to get himself into the seat.

"Eeds, how you gonna get yourself down?" I got more nervous with every move he made. "Let's call your father to help us."

"No, Abs, I can do this. Just give me a minute." He looked down at the seat and took a few deep breaths. "Okay, now I need you to help me."

"What? Tell me."

"Come around here and stand between me and the chair."

"I'm afraid the chair will move," I said.

"Don't worry. You locked it, remember?"

He lifted one arm to let me squeeze between him and the chair. Then he put his free hand on one of my shoulders and then the other one. It was like we were going to dance. I put my hands on his sides. Even through his sweatshirt, I could feel his rib bones sticking out. "Okay, Abs. Now move around slowly until my back is facing the chair." Moving in a circle with baby steps, we gradually turned his body around. When he was at the seat, he let go of me, grabbed the armrests one at a time, and then lowered his body. He was down safely! "Cool, Abs. Thanks."

I put our costumes in Eden's lap and put my hands on the handles of his chair. "I don't know where my strength came from. It was like something inside me just broke open, and suddenly, my arms and legs were doing all the work."

"Maybe that was your anger."

"Yeah, maybe. It's funny. I feel different now, really different. Good though."

"All I can say is I'd better be careful what I say to you from now on," Eden said as I pushed his chair down the street. "Bam, bam, pow, pow, dah, dah, dah, wham!" he said, hunching down to punch the night air like a prizefighter in the middle of a match. I couldn't see his face, but I could sure hear the smile in his voice.

I laughed. A cool night breeze slapped gently against our backs like it was trying to help us get home.

Chapter 13

The next day was Saturday. On weekends my parents usually got up later. I had so much energy that I practically bounced out of bed and crept downstairs to get my own breakfast.

My costume hung on a kitchen chair, looking like someone had yanked the insides out of a body and left the skin behind. It was funny. That was how I usually felt after one of my battles with the pact. Not today though! Today I was bigger, stronger, and in charge of myself all at the same time. It was a cool feeling! I couldn't see it, but I'd bet my smile was huge.

"Hi, honey." My father's slippers scuffed across the kitchen floor behind me. "Got any plans for today?" He pulled the can of coffee and a filter out of the cupboard to make his morning "fix" as he called it.

"Today I get my first laundry lesson. Is Mom up yet?"

"She is." He rested his elbows on the counter next to me. "You know, I don't know a lot about doing laundry," he said in a low voice. "But one thing I noticed is you can do other things while the clothes are being washed or dried. Just thought I'd mention it."

"Got it." I stuck my thumb in the air. "Thanks." He smiled at me as he spooned coffee grounds into the coffeemaker basket.

A few minutes later, my mother entered the kitchen. "All set for your first laundry lesson?" she said, looking directly at me. Her eyes kind of twinkled.

"Yep. All set. See," I said and pointed to my bowl of corn pops. "Extra big breakfast."

By now, the coffee was dripping into the pot. "Let me have some coffee first." She poured herself a cupful and slid onto the stool at the counter. "Speaking of clothes," she said, blowing the steam across the top of her cup, "they're having some great sales at the mall today. It would be a good idea to have you with me since I didn't do so well guessing your size last time. You need some other things for school. How about after we finish the laundry?"

I could see the edges of my father's smile behind his coffee mug.

"Yeah! Where will we go?"

"We'll try Westlake. They have a good selection of stores there," she said before taking a sip of her steaming coffee.

"Cool! I can't wait." I pictured myself walking down the hallway at school, wearing new clothes. Kids shouted at me from wherever they stood. "Cool shoes, Abby." "Hey, Abby, like your new top." That was way out there, I knew. At least I wouldn't have to go around looking like a baby anymore. I mean, if I *wasn't* a baby, why should I dress like one? Things were definitely looking up.

"Okay, the first thing in doing laundry is to collect the clothes and bring them down to the machine," my mother said. "Since you're the new laundry assistant, you can do that while I finish my coffee."

I jumped off the stool and headed for the basement door.

"Abby, clothes are upstairs." She pointed toward the ceiling. "You need something to wash," she said.

"Oh, right." I left the kitchen to get the clothes basket. There was more to this than I thought. You had to kind of plan things. I wasn't sure that I was gonna like this.

✳ ✳ ✳

Saturday afternoon at the mall, I thought of Shelly right away. I don't know what I liked more—shopping or just looking at all the people wandering around under the bright lights. Shelly and I would sometimes sit on a bench and just watch people go by. Even if you didn't buy anything, it was a fun place to be—kind of like a little city under a roof with tons of lights, bright colors, and music. The best part is there is an ocean of people to watch.

This was my first time shopping with my mother. She shopped pretty much like Shelly's mother did. Instead of going slow to look in windows like other people, she charged straight across the mall toward the store she wanted to shop in.

Once we got inside, she headed toward the racks of those shirts that have the little crocodile on them. They had every color you could imagine. It reminded me of the color chart in art class. My mother pulled a pink one off the rack, took it off the hanger, and put it up to my shoulders. "Too small. That's a surprise! You're growing fast." Before today, if I heard her say something like that, a remark would whip across my brain and shoot out of my mouth at her. But here she was spending time doing something for me ... with me. All I could think about was how cool it was to be with her.

She moved her hand along the rack and pulled out a larger size. "Let's try this." Once she got the size down, she said, "What colors do you want?" A choice? I had a choice!

"My favorite color is purple."

"Well, it won't go with your complexion very well," she said. "But you'll probably wear it more because you like the color. What else?" She must have read the surprise on my face. "This is a good sale price, so we should take advantage of it."

By the time we finished in that store, I had seven new tops and two new pairs of jeans, ones that really fit me too. From there we walked across the mall to a shoe store. That was giant surprise number two. I walked out of that store with a new pair of sneakers that had these fake jewels all over them. I only did what she told me. I picked out something like the other girls wore. Even though she didn't really like the ones I had picked, she said okay with no argument or discussion.

On the way home in the car, my mother said, "You know, Abby, if you let your hair grow out a little, we can get a good haircut for you, something that's more flattering. After all, you're in middle school now."

"My hair is like a big ball of curls. How could anyone make it look better?" Learning to talk to my mother and not be sarcastic was harder than I thought. I had to review every remark before I spoke.

"You'd be surprised what a good hairstylist can do. Jeanette is really good, and she knows your hair. We'll ask her." Jeanette had been cutting my hair since I was big enough to get up onto her chair on my own.

When my mother wasn't looking, I dug my nails into my arm. Yep, I was awake. This was real. "Hey, Mom, how about new glasses?" Out of the corner of my eyes, I saw her look over at me.

"How about contacts?" she said. "Then we could see more of your face."

Contacts! I never thought about that. "I don't know if I'd like them."

"Think about it this way," she said. "You wouldn't have those heavy glasses sitting on your nose all the time."

"Hmm." I lifted my glasses up. The dashboard on the car was totally blurred. "Hope they have some strong ones because I can't see anything without these."

"They have whatever strength you need just like glasses. Even different colors."

"You mean I could change my eye color with contacts." I put my glasses back on. Now they felt heavy and old.

"That's what I understand."

"Cool. Like a disguise."

"Not a disguise really." My mother smiled. "Think of it more as an accent to flatter the look that is there already."

Two months ago, I would never have imagined my-self sitting in the car and talking to my mother after we had been on a shopping trip together. Actually, I never imagined that I would stand up to Stephanie either. If you put your mind to it, you could really change a lot of things. Or did things change you? Maybe both. Whatever it was, I liked it all a lot.

✵ ✵ ✵

One thing I noticed about my new clothes was they didn't fold into my body like other outfits I'd worn a lot. When I first put them on, they felt stiff like they were still on the hanger without my body inside them. They smelled nice too like they were coated with fresh air or something. If I didn't move my arms and legs much, maybe my new jeans and top wouldn't lose their stiffness and become worn and old.

It was Monday, three days after I had faced Stephanie. Eden called yesterday to tell me he was all right, just a few scratches on the arm he fell on. When he told his parents he fell out of his chair, they got pretty upset. "I told them you rescued me and helped me get back in the chair. They felt a little better about it, but I don't think I'll be going out at night anytime soon without one of them following behind me. I keep thinking about what you did. You were awesome, Abs. Pow, pow, pow. You got Stephanie to back down."

"I know. It feels good. We'll see what happens when we get to school tomorrow."

"Okay, see you at lunch."

As soon as he hung up, I started to think about how things would go. During the weekend I had decided that when I met her, I would look her right in the eye—not like I was challenging her but just to let her know I meant what I said the other night. I also decided that if she challenged me, I would clench my fists as a way to bring back the courage I felt on Friday night when I finally stood up to her. I'd also make my body rigid like I did then to show I wasn't afraid of her.

After homeroom when I was walking toward math class, I had my first chance to practice. We both arrived at the door of the classroom at the same time. She looked at me but held back like she was fighting to keep in a remark. I locked eyes with her, something I had never had the courage to do before. She looked down her nose at me, trying to make me feel insignificant. But it didn't work! As she made a move to go through the doorway, I cut her off and took myself with my new outfit into the classroom ahead of her.

Later that day she and her group paraded down the hallway toward me just before lunchtime. With her little pack around her, I expected her to feel braver. I turned toward my locker, ready for a comment to fly over my shoulder, maybe a little shove. But there was nothing! They just walked past me down the hallway. Then they laughed, but it didn't bother me as much as it used to. At least they didn't do or say anything to me. I sucked in some air and then let it out, trying to force out the last of the scared feelings from my insides. My shoulders loosened up. This was a totally new feeling! If I needed to, I was ready to stand up to her, to them again. I wasn't afraid. It was like this new girl had come to visit inside me and then decided to stay. I liked her *a lot*!

On the way to lunch, I stopped in the office for my meeting with the principal. I'd never been in the principal's office before. My stomach did this flip-flop thing as I sat waiting for the secretary to tell me he was ready to see me. Suddenly, I wasn't sure if I wanted to go through with it. What if he told me I was making a big deal out of nothing? Then I'd be totally embarrassed. Worse, if he didn't stick up for me and the pack challenged me, I might get into trouble whenever I had to fight back.

"Mr. Winters can see you now, Abby," his secretary said. My stomach did a final flip and continued to flutter all the way down the hallway to his office.

Even though my legs felt heavy, I managed to push them forward along the carpet until they brought me to his door.

When I entered his office, I was surprised at how sunny it was with lots of plants and bright-colored pictures. On a shelf, he had a glass tower with giant bubbles in it that kept moving up toward the top. Mr. Winters came from behind his desk. "Hello, Abby. Have a seat." He waved his hand at the round table near the windows.

I had always seen Mr. Winters at a distance on the school stage or down the hallway. It was funny how someone could seem so much bigger when you met close up. While he shuffled through a pile of things on top of a low bookcase, I glanced at the pictures on the wall above it. They probably showed classes of eighth-graders who had graduated. Someday I'd be up there if I ever made it through this alive. He pulled out a leather-covered pad from the pile and sat opposite me. The knot in his tie formed an almost perfect upside-down colored triangle behind the other triangle made by the edges of his collar.

"What's up? What can I do for you?" He folded his hands on the pad.

It felt like I was about to make a big mistake. But I couldn't just get up and go. I couldn't back out. If I tried to leave, he would probably ask me all kinds of questions and get the information out of me anyway. Principals were supposed to be good at that. "I'm here because I've been having problems since school started with some girls in my grade."

Sunlight bounced off the watch that peeked out from under his shirt cuff. He leaned toward me, interested, all set to listen hard. "What's going on?"

Okay, good so far. "I don't know why, but four girls have been picking on me. I never met them before coming here, and I didn't do anything to them."

"Why did you wait so long to come and tell me?" He flipped the cover of his pad open and started to write. He was taking notes! Was he taking me seriously or writing a note to call my parents and tell them about how weird I was? There was no way to know for sure, so I kept going.

"Be…because I thought that would make it worse." Without thinking about it, my hands folded around the edge of the chair. If only it would take off and take me out of here!

"Worse how?" Every time he asked a question, he looked directly at me. His eyes reminded me of my father's when he tried to help me work out a problem. That relaxed me a little.

"I thought they would come after me for coming to you." His pen scratched across his pad.

"What have they been doing to you?"

"Just about everything—hitting, shoving, tripping, calling me names. One time I got kicked in the ribs …"

His eyes flickered when I said this. "You were kicked in the ribs here at school?" he interrupted. I nodded my head. "Hold on for a second." He got up and went to his desk and punched a button on his phone. "Hi, Jean, come in here, will you? We have a problem I want you to be aware of." He returned to the table.

We waited for a few seconds without talking. Mr. Winters wrote more notes in his pad until the door opened. Ms. Gonzalez, the associate principal, came into the room. Usually, if you got into trouble at school, like a fight or something, you had to report to her. "Jean, this is Abby Wexler. She's been telling me about a problem she's having with some girls in her grade, a group that keeps picking on her, hurting her. I don't recall you telling me anything about it."

"No, this is the first I'm hearing about it." She sat at the table and glued her eyes to my face.

"Abby tells me that these girls have been shoving and hitting her. One time they kicked her in the ribs."

He waited. Ms. Gonzalez's eyes got really big like two dark marbles sitting at the top of her cheeks.

Mr. Winters turned back to me. "All right, so they've been doing these things to you during the school day."

"Yes. They threatened to keep on making my life miserable. Even after Eden and I won the social studies prize—"

"Eden Gray," he asked.

"Yes. After we won the prize, they told me they'd come after me if Eden didn't tell you that he did all the work on the project and I did nothing. They even tried to damage the project before the judges came around, but Eden caught them."

"Abby says this has been going on since school started," he said to Ms. Gonzalez.

"You've been putting up with this without telling anyone here at school, none of the teachers or counselors," Ms. Gonzalez asked.

"I … I was afraid they'd come after me again if I told." At least they weren't telling me that it was no big deal. They were actually taking me seriously.

"What changed your mind," Ms. Gonzalez asked.

"The other night Eden and I met them on our street after trick-or-treating. The leader attacked Eden, and his wheelchair fell over. Then she squeezed his neck so hard he couldn't breathe. It made me so mad that I jumped on her, got her off Eden, and told her I was tired of it all. I also told her I would come to you and tell you about everything that was going on. So that's why I'm here."

Ms. Gonzalez and Mr. Winters glanced at each other with a look of surprise or shock. Then they turned back to me.

"Okay, have you seen any of these girls today," Mr. Winters asked. "Have they tried anything?"

"I met the leader one time and then all of them before lunch, but they didn't do anything."

"Okay, Abby, here's what has to happen." Mr. Winters gripped his pen with both hands. "Ms. Gonzalez and I will talk to Eden Gray beforehand, and then we'll call these four girls down to the office. We will talk with them one at a time and go over everything you told us to get each one's reaction to it. It's likely they'll deny any of it ever happened, but I'm going to warn them that if we get any more reports about any one of them doing anything else like this here at school or on the bus to you or any other student, then there will be consequences. We're also going to contact their parents about this."

Parents! Oh, man, all of a sudden, this got very big very fast. "Do you have to … tell their parents?"

He nodded. "Yes, I have to share this with them. Most parents don't want their children doing things like this. Besides, if these girls bother other students off school grounds, we can't do anything about it, but their parents can. Is that a problem?"

"I guess." I picked at my fingernails and looked away from him.

"How do your parents feel about all this," Ms. Gonzalez asked. "I haven't heard from them." She looked at Mr. Winters, who shook his head. "Neither of us has."

"They don't know." That sounded strange, kind of like admitting *I* did something wrong.

"What you just told us is true, right," Ms. Gonzalez asked.

I looked straight at her. "Yes."

"Then why didn't you tell them?" Her eyebrows wrinkled up.

I didn't want it to sound like my parents didn't care about what happened to me. "Because I thought they would make a big deal out of it, and I thought it would only get worse for me." I shoved my hands under my legs on the seat of the chair.

"So basically, you suffered in silence for two months," Mr. Winters said.

"At first, I did. But then Eden figured it out, and

we tried to take care of it ourselves. That didn't work. Then when I saw the bossy one attack Eden the other night, I decided I had to come and talk to you." I watched my shoes swing back and forth and hit in the middle.

"I'm sorry this happened to you, Abby, and I wish you had come to us sooner. We could have helped you. Not only do we want you to be happy here in middle school, but we also need to be sure you're safe. All right, here comes the hard part. I need their names." He held his pen up over the pad.

This part was going to be hard. Once their names were out, I couldn't take them back. Then this whole thing would grow like one of those fall windstorms that left a big mess of broken branches in your yard before it took off to do more damage somewhere else. That was what happened when your parents or teachers got involved in stuff. But I couldn't get rid of the picture in my mind of Stephanie choking Eden the other night. It was time to be honest and admit I couldn't fix it by myself. Besides, even if the pack did stop bothering me, that didn't mean they wouldn't go after someone else. Maybe they already were. What if they seriously hurt some other kid because I messed up this chance to stop it? Thinking about that scared me a lot.

Suddenly, their names came rushing out of my mouth, one after the other. I pulled my hands from beneath my legs and sat back in the chair. Afterward, I was a little tired. Then this feeling came over me, not calmness exactly. I was still a little shaky. It felt more like when you just finished a test that was really hard. Yeah, I felt lighter. Whatever happened, the hard part was over. Or that was what I thought. Until Mr. Winters laid a bomb on me.

"Good girl. Now here's the next thing you have to do." Mr. Winters bent his shoulders toward me. He laid his pen on the pad. "You have to tell your parents, and you have to do it tonight."

I looked out the window away from his face as he continued. "They'll be upset at first because, like us, they always want to know that you are safe. But they'll understand when you tell them why you waited. And you have to tell them to call me so that I know you've done this part. That's very important. Understand? If I haven't heard from them by tomorrow morning at ten o'clock, I will call them. Most parents don't like to have the school call them at work, so you do your job tonight, okay?"

I nodded even though I didn't want to do it. Things were going so well right now, especially with my mom. I didn't want to wreck that.

I left Mr. Winters' office and found Eden in the lunchroom. "Where you been? I was beginning to get worried about you."

"Mr. Winters' office." I set my tray on the table and flopped into the chair across from him.

"You did it? You told him? How did it go?"

"It was okay until he told me he wants me to tell my parents."

"So?" He put a potato chip in his mouth. Of course, he wouldn't see any problem with that.

"Well, I just don't know what they'll say."

When I took a bite of my sandwich, it dropped like a rock into my stomach. The knot was back. Funny how things could change from great to terrible in a millisecond.

* * *

On the bus ride home, all the reasons I could think of about why my parents should not get upset with me swirled around in my brain. I was the one who got beat up. I told the truth. I was their only daughter. I was their only smart daughter who won a big prize for my project. I helped out around the house. I didn't get into trouble at school. I always did my homework. The list could get very long. But I knew none of those things would make much difference when it came to this. The fact was that I didn't tell them, and they weren't going to like that. The worst thing was I couldn't get out of it now because Mr. Winters was waiting to get a call from them.

At supper my parents were talking about the change in the weather, and my father was going to start looking for a new snow blower. My world was falling apart piece by piece while my father explained to my mother the benefits of a rider mower over a push model. I had to remind myself, though, that he had no reason to be worried about me since I always said that I was *fine* whenever he asked me how I was. But I had to get this out now before I lost my courage. So, when he handed me the dish of string beans, I blurted out, "Guys, I have to tell you about something that happened to me at school." Both of them stopped talking and looked at me.

"What's so urgent that you couldn't wait for us to finish?" my mother asked. She always insisted that it was rude to interrupt a conversation.

"I've been having a problem at school with some kids who have been bothering me." I put down the bowl of green beans and slid my hands under my legs.

My father looked at my mother and then said, "Explain what you mean by problem. What were they doing to you?" He put his fork down on his plate and folded his arms on the edge of the table.

"They were like pushing, shoving, hitting me. You know, that kind of stuff." I tried to look at him, but I couldn't.

"Pushing, shoving, hitting," he said. "Kids at school have been pushing, shoving, and hitting you!" his voice got louder with each word. "For how long?"

I looked down at my lap. "Since school started."

"That's almost ... two months!" He sat back fast. He sounded surprised and angry at the same time, but I couldn't tell who he was angry at. "This has been going on for more than two months, and you didn't tell us. I don't understand. Why didn't the teachers do something about it or call us. What about the principal?"

"They didn't know. They didn't see it," I shot a sideways look at him to be sure he got that point.

"How can that be?" My father looked at my mother again. "What kind of a school are they running down there?"

"Wait, Bob," my mother said as she placed her hand on his arm. "Abby, why couldn't they see what was going on?" I was glad she asked that. Now I could explain.

"Because these girls did it when there was always

a crowd of kids around," I said. "Like in the hallway at change of classes."

"But weren't the teachers there? Why didn't they see them," my mother asked.

"The one time a teacher called them on it, they lied and said it was an accident, and they stuck up for one another. Other times they did it in a place where they couldn't be seen like when no one was in the hallway or in a stairway where the doors were closed."

"So, we've got kids roughing up our daughter, and no one knows it's going on?" my father said to my mother. "Great!" His face got redder every time he heard something new.

"Alright, so they followed you into an empty place and then what?" My mother ignored his comment and kept pushing for the facts.

"They didn't follow me. They surrounded me and pushed me into the stairwell." My mother blinked when I said that. "In the hallway they always say embarrassing things about me loud enough for the other kids to hear them. But in the stairway when they called me names and I didn't fight back, they hit me really hard."

"Why? Why you?" my mother asked. "What is it about you that makes them want to hurt you?"

"I never even knew them before middle school. I

don't know why they decided to pick on me. I never did anything to any of them. They're bigger than I am. Why would I try to make them angry at me on purpose?"

"Abby, why didn't you tell us before now," my mother asked.

I ran my finger along the edge of the table. I wondered how they were going to react to this. "Because I thought you'd make a big deal about it. I thought it would get worse"

"Why should we make a big deal out of a group of kids brutalizing our daughter in school?" my father said like he was asking an audience that wasn't in the room. "I can't imagine why."

"What do you mean worse," my mother asked. She was the calm one. I thought it would be the other way around.

"I mean if you talked to the principal and he talked to them, then they would come after me again and hurt me worse." She kept her eyes on me.

"So, what changed your mind." she asked. "Why did you finally tell us?"

If I told them about the other night, my father would get so upset he'd probably take off for their houses right then. But I had to tell them the whole story about the girls coming up to us the other night and attacking Eden and injuring him and how I fought Stephanie.

My father said, "So Eden's the only one who knew it was going on?"

"Until today when I told Mr. Winters, the principal. He told me I had to tell you."

"Well, believe me—he and a few more people up there have a lot of explaining to do. We send you to school every day expecting that at the very least you'll to be safe, and what happens? You get beaten up." He was pounding the table with his finger now. "What's wrong with this picture?" His hands were flying all over the place as he spoke.

"See, Dad. That's what I mean!" In a split second, my mood changed from afraid to angry. "You're getting all worked up, and you'll probably go down to school and holler at the principal and teachers. Then I'll be embarrassed. I won't be able to show my face in school again!" I glared at him.

His eyes got really narrow. "Listen to me, young lady. You have a lot more explaining to do. How do you think this makes us feel, telling the principal before telling us? Is it possible you think we don't care what happens to you?"

"Bob, hold on," my mother warned. "Abby's right. You're getting too excited."

"Too excited! Too excited! My daughter was beaten up, and I didn't know about it. I couldn't do anything about it because I had no idea it was going on."

"Our daughter," my mother reminded him as she gently put a hand on his arm. "And you're right. We couldn't help her because we didn't know about it. But going on like this isn't helping anything right now, is it?" Her voice was pretty even. I knew she was trying to bring him down from his angry place.

My father looked at her and then me and then back at her. He took a deep breath. "No, I guess not."

"What we have to do now is figure out what to do from here on in, right?" She was still talking to him.

"I know. I know," he said. "But I have one more thing to say before we go there." He looked at me and said, "I'm disappointed you didn't tell us first. I thought you trusted us." Something about the way he said that told me he wasn't angry exactly. It was more like he was hurt.

"I'm sorry, Dad. All I can say is I thought they'd hurt me more if I did." I looked down at the lines in my hands.

"There is *no way* I would let that happen. Do you hear me? It would *not* happen again." Yeah, that was pretty clear. Now he was back at angry but not at me now. He laid his hand on the table, turned it up, and pushed it over toward me.

I knew that meant he wanted me to put my hand in his, so I did. When I looked up at him, his eyes were watery. Oh, my god, he was going to cry! I never expected that! "I'm okay now, Dad."

"But you almost weren't." He squeezed my hand.

"I think your father and I had better make an appointment with Mr. Winters," my mother said, looking over at me.

I nodded my head.

"Before we talk to him, do we need any more information about these two girls?" she asked.

"Four. There were four of them," I said.

"Four?" she said. "Four of them against one of you!"

I nodded. She looked directly at me, and right away, I saw a change come over her face. She was having a hard time with that. She did this quick shake of her head as if she was trying to make the idea of what I said fit into her head, but it wouldn't work. "Okay." She cleared her throat and folded her napkin, put it carefully on the table next to her plate, and patted it twice. Then she stood up. "I'm going to leave a message on the principal's answering machine." Her voice had this high pitch like she was forcing herself not to scream. She kept talking as she headed toward the kitchen phone like someone on a mission. "I know they're not there now, but I want that to be the first message the secretary gets in the morning." She pointed her finger in the air and said, "We are going down there tomorrow."

My father and I followed her with our eyes. When she disappeared into the kitchen, he turned to me. "You know, honey, if you had told us sooner, it might not have gotten as bad as it did. When were you going to tell us?"

I wiggled. I was hoping he wouldn't ask that question. "I don't know."

"You mean you would have let them continue to do this to you ... until when?"

With my other hand, I rubbed the handle of my fork. "I guess I kept hoping it would stop, that they'd pick on someone else and leave me alone."

"But they could have hurt you even more before that happened. What if we didn't find out about this until you landed in the hospital? Imagine how we'd have felt then."

I never thought about that. Then I had this sudden flashback of Eden lying on the ground and Stephanie choking him. What if she had hurt him so bad that he had to be taken to the hospital ... or worse? How would I have explained that to his parents, to mine? This was kind of a mess.

"Doesn't sound like a very good plan, honey. You

know, there's a difference between them calling you names and physically hurting you."

I pictured myself in the corridor before school two months ago, listening to the pack make loud comments about my clothes or my size or how dumb I was. I saw myself walking by all the kids who heard those things and felt them looking at me and laughing behind my back. The pain of being embarrassed like that hurt from the top of my head all the way down to my toes. For me, it hurt more than being kicked in the ribs.

My mother came back to the table. "I put a message on the principal's machine. Was it always four girls who attacked you?"

"Mostly, once or twice there were just three," I said.

"How often did it happen?" She put a pad down on the table in front of her and clicked the pen she held.

"Two or three times."

"All right, two or three times a week these girls were doing something like hitting you or calling you names." She wrote as she talked.

"No, Mom, two or three times a day," I said, looking straight at her.

She stopped writing and looked up at me. Her mouth dropped open. "This happened two or three times *a day?*"

I nodded.

"What are their names?" She looked sideways at my father. "I think we should call their parents." Of course, he shook his head yes.

Oh man, things had just cooled down. Now they were heating up again. I could imagine my father and mother yelling into the phone or worse, going to their houses. Then I pictured my father grabbing one of the fathers by the collar and shoving him against his front door.

"No, wait, Mom, Dad. Talk to Mr. Winters first. He said today he was going to call their parents. Wait till you talk to him tomorrow."

My mother said, "Maybe you're right." She slapped the pen onto the pad. "This is so upsetting. Someone was hurting you, and we couldn't help you because we didn't know. Why would they do that, go around hurting other kids for no reason? I don't get it."

I raised my shoulders and let them fall. "Believe me, Mom, I've gone over everything I've done since school started, and there's nothing I could think of."

"Getting a kick out of hurting other people—it just doesn't make sense." She was searching inside her own head for an answer that wasn't there.

"Nothing I've heard tonight makes sense," my father said. "I hope one thing is clear to you," he said, looking at me. "From now on, if someone tries to hurt you, I ..." He looked at my mother and continued, "We need to know that you will tell us right away the *first* time it happens. Promise us that."

"I'll try, Dad."

"Not good enough," he said. This was a part of my dad I never knew existed. He was so angry about me getting hurt and him not being there to protect me from harm. I always figured he would take care of me, but I never knew how much it meant to him. Until now! Both of them were ready to fight for me. Funny how things that happened to you helped you learn things about your parents that you never knew before.

"Yeah, okay, first time it happens." Man, was I tired. I excused myself from the table and went upstairs to my room. The fact that I had not eaten anything did not seem to matter.

✳ ✳ ✳

My parents met with Mr. Winters and Ms. Rodriguez the next morning. I sat in a chair outside the office because my parents said that I had been through enough and that they didn't think I had to be there. When they came out, my father put his hands on my shoulders and said, "You won't have any more problems with them from now on." Then he kissed my forehead. I had a feeling from the way he said it that it was true.

That night my mother told me that I didn't have to worry about being embarrassed because my father did not holler at anyone. That was all they said about it, and I was just as glad. All I wanted was for it to be over.

When I got off the bus in the morning, it seemed like a different place for me. I actually looked forward to being at school. The best thing was that if the pack ever bothered me again, I had backup, protection. I was not scared anymore.

Mr. Gibson shared with us our grade for the first quarter. I got an A. Handing in my own math solutions to him must have helped. That gave me the courage to consider answering in class.

After school Eden and I met to do homework together and to sketch out a plan for our science project. Things started to feel a little more normal, kind of like they did when Shelly was here but better because I felt good about myself. I smiled as I walked back down the ramp to my house.

If I had to give this first quarter in middle school a grade, it would be a D minus, about as bad as it could have been but not a total failure. Things were starting to improve. I was thinking pretty seriously about trying out for basketball as a way to make my-self—what was that term my mother used the other day—*well balanced?* Then I reminded myself that I'd rather sit and do something where I have to think in a quiet way like chess club instead of being more physical like in basketball. That decided it for me. I'm going to do what felt right for me from now on, not what helped me fit in. I'd be the one to decide where I fit in. It was settled. I'd join chess then, or the Science Explorers Club or photography. I felt like I had more options now that I knew myself better. Cool!

About the Author

M.M. Murray was a classroom teacher and reading specialist at the primary, middle school, and junior high school levels. She currently lives in West Hartford, Connecticut.

CPSIA information can be obtained
at www.ICGtesting.com
Printed in the USA
BVHW03s0213090718
521151BV00001B/44/P

9 781480 863187